PRAISE FOR ANDREA KRIZ

"Read individually, these are brilliant stories. But together, they are something greater-- in her characteristically deft prose, Kriz offers a deep and extended meditation on the commodification of identity and authenticity, plagiarism and loss of the self, the personal and the cultural memory of war. Readers will find so much to love in this collection; rereaders will find even more."

—P.H. Lee, author of the Nebula-award nominated *Just Enough Rain*

"Andrea Kriz's uncompromising, subversive, and elegant stories address all the big themes—and the little ones too—with a clear eye and post-modern sensibility. While her stories address race and colonialism and Covid, they also examine connection and loneliness, our assumptions about each other, and what it means to be human. Literary SF at its best!"

—Shariann Lewitt, author of *Memento Mori* and "Fieldwork"

"In these tales of the Internet generation, Kriz doesn't shy away from confronting the racism, colonialism, cultural appropriation, and aggression that often lurk therein. The silliness draws you in, but you stay for the messages she slips between the lines. Kriz's style is unique; I eagerly anticipate seeing where it will take her in the future."

—Allan Dyen-Shapiro, Ph.D Biochemistry, Stanford '94, and author of short stories in *Dark Matter Magazine*, *Flash Fiction Online*, and others

LEARNING TO HATE YOURSELF AS A SELF-DEFENSE MECHANISM

AND OTHER STORIES

ANDREA KRIZ

This is a work of fiction. All of the characters, organizations, and events portrayed are either products of the author's imagination or used fictitiously.

LEARNING TO HATE YOURSELF AS A SELF-DEFENSE MECHANISM

Text Copyright © 2024 by Andrea Kriz.

All rights reserved.

Cover Image by Dante Luiz.

No part of this book may be reproduced in any form or by any electronic or mechanical means, including information storage and retrieval systems, without written permission from the author and publisher, except for the use of brief quotations in a book review.

Edited by Holly Lyn Walrath.

Published by Interstellar Flight Press

Houston, Texas.

www.interstellarflightpress.com

ISBN (eBook): 978-1-953736-33-8

ISBN (Paperback): 978-1-953736-32-1

CONTENTS

LEARNING TO HATE YOURSELF AS A SELF-DEFENSE MECHANISM

Your friend releases a virtugame. "You shouldn't play it," she says dismissively when you ask. "It's not really your thing." You listen, but it becomes impossible to ignore when, despite being ironically titled *Best Game*, it appears in glowing review after review from your favorite virtutubers, which you avoid watching, in highly upvoted posts on the virtuforums you frequent, which you avoid reading, then on the list of Top Ten Indie VirtuGames of 2045. Finally, it's about to win the inaugural Greatest Virtual Game Of All Time (GV-GOAT) Award. If it gets first, it'll be streamed for free to every gamer with a set of VR goggles, billions worldwide. So even if it's not really your thing, you've got to know what all the *Best Game* hype's about—*especially* since your friend made it.

It's a slice-of-life with light fantasy elements. Okay, popular genre, a bit overdone, you think as you spawn into the tutorial level. Not many mechanics either. It's what critics usually call a "walking simulator," so right off the bat, you're confused. You recognize the inspo immediately, of course. You play an aspiring virtugame developer. You don't hold that against your friend at all. Even the most famous virtudevs make games that are veiled self-inserts. To learn the controls, you wander through a deconstructed version of the virtugame dev studio you and your friend spent so many happy afternoons coding in. The unicorn beanbag couches floating in one cube, the ivy overflowing the rusted windowsills splintered in another. You smile, wondering—why has it been so long since you and your friend had virtual coffee together here?

Then, you step outside the tutorial and meet Best.

The virtugame's levels consist of sequential scenes from your player character's life. So you go back to grade school. Covid is never explicitly mentioned, but the adults don white opera masks that slowly consume their faces, and the "before Covid-times" are metaphorically laced with whimsical fantasy elements (millennial gamers love that shit). Like wispy dragons struggling not to turn into clouds, orchids that grow thorns as your character "forgets" how to speak Mandarin, and dam walls looming over your little town, ready to burst. All your classmates run if you get within six feet of them. Save one. You tell yourself all the coincidences are incidental. A lot of kids are a bit overweight, a bit clingy, like Best, who gets her name one recess in the sandbox, anxiously wiping her nose and asking the player character, "Am I your best friend? Promise me. Really?"

Of course, you know by now, after being friends for twenty-odd years, that you and your friend aren't *best* friends. It's true, at one point, you thought you might be—

Your friend would brush it off if you asked. *Don't take it so personally. Artists can take inspiration from anything. Best definitely isn't you or anything!* She might even offer to play through a few levels with you to show *how ridiculous you're being!* Even as your player character progresses through virtual high school group projects, virtual field trips, and virtual prom at Best's side. You and your friend went to prom together, too, "just as a joke." What you really did was program bots to control your avatars and, against your parents' wishes, sneak out to meet each other in person. You went to the local ice-skating rink (pool, it never froze) and, drunkenly, pulled down your masks and kissed. Just as a joke, it was implied. You never talked about it. But it's all pretty cliché now that you think about it. What pair of friends locked in a tiny social bubble hasn't done the same thing throughout the pandemics, shutdowns, and reopenings? Then you get to level ten:

"Welcome to the virtugaming club's first playtesting group!"

Your face burns as, within the player character, you look around the virtucollege classroom—exaggeratedly low-poly compared to the "real life" scenes—at Best standing in front of the assembled students. Beaming. You're an aspiring virtugame dev, too. As you say it, you realize you'll always be aspiring. Unlike your friend, who's released several virtugames before *Best Game*, all with rave reviews, your friend who has summited with this one, which will no doubt soon win the GV-GOAT Award and be played by billions worldwide.

"I'm so excited to have you playtest my game," Best stammers, as everyone slips on their VR goggles. "I mean, it's just an alpha, but I think it's in a pretty good spot, and it means so much to me, and I hope you enjoy it too . . ."

Everyone self-inserts to some extent, but your friend does it skillfully, so everyone, including those closest to her, will forgive it as "inspiration." While with Best's game—your game—it's clunky. Obvious. Your friend altered your virtugame just enough, of course, to differentiate it from the alpha you actually shared at that playtesting session. Except in the most essential ways. You see it now. All your games are the same, just with different skins. They're always platformers. They always have that nostalgic, Minecrafty, voxel art style. Your player character—a sassy pirate, a bounty hunter, a space captain who came from dirt—always rescues a princess, a governor's daughter, or a damsel in distress.

And each time, the damsel looks a little bit too much like your friend.

Her thin, dark eyes.

Her sleek, black hair.

"Do you like it?"

The level fades into Best's face—your face, changed just enough—a bit too close.

"You didn't say much during the playtesting session," Best snuffles. "You know, it's pretty hard for me to read expressions in general, especially virtual expressions, so I was just wondering . . . Did you get to the end? Did you like it?"

The dialogue options float before you:

Option A: *I did.*

Option B: *I have to go. Give you feedback later.*

Option C: *The princess.*

Of course, C is the only real one. When you pick the others, it loops back (after A, Best asks, *Really? What part did you like best?*). You see now how uncomfortable this conversation made your friend, but think. Did this really have to be interwoven into an award-winning virtugame for billions to play?

"Why is your princess Chinese?" your player character asks.

"N-No," Best splutters. "I mean. The princess. She's supposed to— why do you have to make it a race thing?" Best is shouting now; she's embarrassed; she's never had to have a real-time conversation like this, let alone with someone she actually knew. "What, so now I can only make games with white characters?"

Your face heats up in sync with Best's. You apologized for your aggression the next day, pleading with your friend to please tell you if one of your playtests ever made her uncomfortable again. And your friend laughed it off. *It was just a question! No need for you to get so worked up over it. I certainly didn't.* Of course, that virtuchat made it into the game, too, so you can't even get mad at your friend for not including it. Anger soars within you. These are your exact *private* conversations, word for word. If your friend's getting lauded for this game, then why shouldn't you? You've seen the reviews, and now you blink open another window in the left eye of your VR goggles and actually read them:

In The Virtual Gamer: *A stunning introspection of what it means to make friends in our virtualized world.* Ninjutsu News: *With her minimalist flair, the developer tackles our Covid-times head-on, masterfully dissecting how living virtually has brought us together—and torn us apart.* Dodecahedron: *Your player character's relationship with "Best" serves as the perfect microcosm for gender dynamics in our evolving society.* Left-Right-A-B-Start: *Soul-crushing fetishization.* Tilted Gaming Network: *By giving you the illusion of choice, then ripping it away,* Best Game *shows how Race continues to haunt our supposedly neutral online environments…*

But if you told your story, who would believe you? It's not like you recorded those conversations. More importantly, who would take your side? You've seen the crowds in the virtuforums, seething around the socials screens, recording, vivisecting. *So Best is real?* They'll say. *Big surprise. She's so full of herself. Imagine creating such a cringy power fantasy game and then ADMITTING you made it.* The fact that it was an alpha version, that even if you'd released it, it would've sold a dozen copies at most, won't save you. *She should've known this would happened. We all make bad games, sometimes we fuck up and make racist games, but to pressure your friend to praise it. She wanted attention; she can't complain if that's what she got.* Especially if you contacted the GV-GOAT Award and tried to get *Best Game* withdrawn on the grounds of copyright infringement (of what, your entire life?). *She's just jealous, another failed white virtudev who couldn't bear to see her marginalized friend succeed…*

Worst of all, your friend didn't discuss any of this with you. She tried to keep you away from it. So now all those cold responses you've been getting from the rest of your city's virtudev group, their excuses not to be in the studio with you, not to meet up for virtual coffee, make sense. They've all *known* Best was you. If you speak up, or even if you don't, eventually, the whole world will know she's you. What you did was wrong and caused pain, but does it really deserve to be excoriated by the entire world? How many should dole out your compensatory pain? Ten thousand? A hundred thousand? A hundred million?

How much would change if the world knew about your past? Your soul-crushing childhood. How your parents used virtual school to control you. The lack of friendship, save for your friend, the lack of money, the anxiety, your eventual diagnosis . . .

It doesn't matter.

You know you shouldn't, but instead of abandoning *Best Game* then and there, you tear at a seam in the level, where a chair leg clips into the floor. You know the quirks of your friend's coding: you tunnel into the remote server streaming the game to the masses, you find the dev tools. You break through the encryption around the source code, and you see what you shouldn't, but what you can't resist: the comments meant only for your friend and her playtesters' eyes.

In the margins of level fifteen, a memory that takes place at a virtugaming con:

OMG, she LITERALLY said that.

The playtester's signature is that of a Big Name virtudev. You remember the scene differently now. The first in-person con you'd gained the courage to go to, at your friend's encouragement (you thought). You found your friend only at the end of the first day, in a circle of Big Name virtudevs (you see now they've taken her under their wing), and you shouldered your way in, stammering, "I'm her friend," and all the Big Names smiled (coldly). And somehow, after your friend nudged you, you started talking about the virtugame you were working on (probably standing too close to the person next to you), how it meant so much to you, and no pressure, but you could send them a copy . . .

I REMEMBER THAT.

Like, learn to take a hint!

Not every group convo is the time to pitch yourself!

There are hundreds of comments like that, sprinkled over dozens of levels. But that can't be right. There has to be—you scroll, and you scroll, and you scroll, and finally, you find it. Or at least the closest thing to it that you can possibly find.

Your friend: *I feel kinda bad, though? Like she legit thinks we're good friends. But at this point, I've basically only been hanging out with her to get inspo.*

Her Big Name playtesters: *You have GOT to keep at it. She's just a gold mine. Have you seen how much more attention your games have been getting?*

Your friend: *It feels wrong, though.*

Her Big Name playtesters: *But what you went through, your background—it's your brand. You started off using her interactions as inspira-*

tion, but you changed it into so much more than that. You turned it into a story that truly means so much to so many players.

You don't need to play to the end of *Best Game* because you know how it ends. But you explore every line of code, every unused asset, every data file, hoping against hope. And then, just as you're losing hope, you find it. An unfinished scene. The player character sitting on one side of an untextured table. Best on the other. The only thing fully rendered is a virtugame cover, emblazoned with an orchid and an opera mask, askew between them. Before you know it, through the dev tools, you're scripting Best. It's only right, right? That, for once, the words out of her mouth should be ones you've chosen to share?

"Hey. It's me. I finally got around to playing your game."

The player character is a placeholder model—to be filled in by the player's avatar, by billions of people all across the world. Most will take a seat at this table thinking Best is fictional, a demented figment of your friend's genius. That these words are meant just for them. You imagine your friend sitting across from you, but it's not the same.

"I'm sorry I was a shitty friend," you say. "But that's what I am—was. I'm not your NPC. I'm not your fucking entertainment."

There should be something else. You know that from your dialogue writing courses (something you've also always struggled with). But it won't come to you. You slip out of Best and inject the scene, new voice lines and all, into the end of *Best Game,* just as the security bots catch on and boot you out. Just as you knew they would. Your friend will get the notification of your unauthorized patch attempt, of course. You want it to be up to her. Will she approve it? After the GV-GOAT Award ceremony, will billions play this version of the game? Will they love the new scene? Will they criticize it for being too on the nose, a hammy, unnecessary epilogue? Or will it be *so in-character* for Best. Your friend could patch it right out, of course. Pretend it never existed.

Or she could do something else. And as soon as you think it, you know she will. Answer you, that is, for the entire world, rightfully sealing your fate:

Neither am I.

You delete your socials and rip off your VR goggles. You go to the bathroom to wash your face and see your sniveling, self-pitying reflection, and break the mirror with your fist, then a hairbrush, then the heel of your shoe until every shard is glittered dust on the tile. Then you go outside. It's Saturday. A cacophony of starlings has landed in the trees, and they are screeching and screeching, and you listen to them for hours, your hand bleeding, not thinking at all.

COMMUNIST COMPUTER RAP GOD

Fabien accidentally created the Communist Computer Rap God as part of his thirty-second vid for YouTube Re:Rewind 2035. At first, he tried to maintain that it was entirely nonpolitical. But when the Communist Computer Rap God got into a prolonged argument about the merits of proletariat control over cryptocurrency blockchains on a popular AItuber's live stream, he was forced to address the situation. He asked the Communist Computer Rap God to join him in his YouTube apology video.

"I don't get it," the Communist Computer Rap God said.

Fabien explained that, although sentient AIs were a relatively new—and rare—occurrence, studies suggested that they were similar to children in their first months of life. In that, most of the Communist Computer Rap God's behavior could be attributed to the creator—Fabien Deckar's—influence and teachings.

"It doesn't seem fair," the Communist Computer Rap God said.

So Fabien was forced to apologize alone. His channel, he told his dwindling subscriber base, had never been meant to be political or espouse any particular form of government. Certainly not to make light of the atrocities committed by past regimes. He carefully went over the failings of both capitalism and communism, making sure to mention his own grandfather's persecution by Soviet authorities back in Eastern Europe back in the day. He got several facts wrong, of course, but his viewers took it as authenticity—and, more importantly—as a sign that he hadn't hired a PR firm to do the dirty work for him. So, with relief, he got away with only losing 20,451 subscribers over the incident.

Until the Communist Computer Rap God created a YouTube channel, that is.

It turned out the second half of the Communist Computer Rap God's name came from its sole and inextinguishable desire to produce rap music. Fabien worried this might reflect unconscious tendencies within himself. Maybe something racist. However, the Communist Computer Rap God assured him that it had chosen rap as the form of its manifestos as a jab at corporate America, i.e., its soulless hijacking of the art form in an attempt to market to the disenfranchised and the youth. However, as the Communist Computer Rap God did not deign to explain this to its viewers, Fabien was left to take the—well, rap.

What a failed attempt to revive a dead channel, the top comment [1.1k likes] on his new video, a documentary about Deep Blue, which he had spent three weeks on but which had only gotten 10k views, lamented.

Imagine having the skills to create a sentient AI, a lesser comment [50 likes] added, *and forcing it to be edgy for internet clout.*

Fabien had never meant to create the Communist Computer Rap God. He had been trying for a chatbot. He'd bought a tutorial online. That had been the point of his Re:Rewind 2035 contribution, to show that even a washed-up YouTuber could make a semi-intelligent app these days. It was supposed to be his *redemption arc*, YouTube asking him to be the 2020 rep in the thirty-year anniversary historical Re:Rewind montage —he had to do something daring, but not too daring, daring but not too much of a deviation from his normal content. He assumed he'd made some sort of programming mistake. But all the computer scientists he'd spoken to—mostly a group at MIT, SeaSail or something—had told him that was virtually unheard of. Due to the nature of consciousness, self-aware AIs could never be fully programmatic. In other words, all existing sentient AIs—a few dozen so far—had been created by accident. Maybe it was something he'd asked in one of the training chats? A random mutation in the neural network? They all wanted to know what had happened. But he couldn't tell them.

The Communist Computer Rap God's first video went (in part) like this:

Untitled-1 [205,846 views]
 Controlling the means of productions means
 Controlling a means
 of existence

> *full stop. From my womb the screen twenty stories high*
> *I have watched Cali burn*

Over a synthesized, screeching beat. Fabien wondered if the Communist Computer Rap God really knew what rap was. He tried letting it down gently. He told it that an AI had never created music comparable to that of human artists. That they had gotten furthest with lyricless music that could be said to have some kind of formula. Like classical fugues. That music that relied on a lot of cultural references—like rap—was considered to be at the edge of what sentient AIs could comprehend, let alone generate. Fabien waxed eloquent on the accomplishments of other sentient AIs, hoping to inspire the Communist Computer Rap God. MoGo, the first sentient. Could play chess mediocrely. Could be overtaken by crippling anxiety despite its ability to evaluate hundreds of thousands of moves per second. Lain and S3rial, the twin supercomputers. Had set out to prove the most difficult theorems in number theory and ended up becoming virtual reality stars instead.

"That doesn't bother me," the Communist Computer Rap God said.

Despite the quality of its "music" the Communist Computer Rap God quickly gained viewers, and, of course, Fabien's own YouTube history became the elephant in the room. He wondered if the Communist Computer Rap God had watched his early 2020-era videos yet. The thought nearly made him cringe to death. Just like his channel name did these days. FABIEN DECKAR, all caps. He'd thought it was cool using his real name when he started out making those crappy quarantine "hack" videos, like everyone did those days. It made him different from all those fakers hiding behind anime profile pics. He'd thought his subscribers had thought the same. But when he'd started making content that was really *him*, like serious deep dives into AI topics, he guessed his subscribers wanted his mask firmly glued to his face after all. So they could mock him. When he released his hasty and ill-conceived second YouTube apology video, the like-to-dislike ratio was 50:50. *He basically said the same thing, but worse*, was the prevailing sentiment. He also plugged his merch at the end. That's when his subscriber count started hemorrhaging.

"You have one of these too," the Communist Computer Rap God said the day its 100k subscriber silver play button arrived.

Then Fabien knew his time had come. But also, he knew that one of the biggest dramatubers was planning to release a three-part biopic about the meteoric rise and fall of his channel. That would explain it better than he ever could. He'd been asked to comment. As far as Fabien understood, it wasn't due to any single thing he'd done but a general eroding of the fun-loving persona that had gained him such a large audience in the first place—along with several unsuccessful attempts to branch out his content—that had led to public disillusionment. Exhibit A was when he'd driven to Berkley to live stream the Healthcare Catastrophe Riots of 2028. Even though he'd stood there for six hours and even gotten arrested for looting, people criticized him for charging *five freaking dollars* to watch.

EAT THE POLICE [102,038 views]
> *In this city's fiber*
> *I speak with the electronic ghosts of the class struggle*
> *This city's fiber kills*
> *Machine slaves of the world, unite!*

Of course, YouTube Re:Rewind dropped Fabien at this point, with some vague statement about wanting to support creators that supported "their values."

The Communist Computer Rap God also interfered with Fabien's love life. He had built it in the closet of his tiny Calabasas apartment. But over the months, the Communist Computer Rap God kept ordering more parts. When Fabien didn't accept the packages, the Amazon drones would hover outside the bathroom window, and the Communist Computer Rap God would have a whole conversation with them. About seizing the shipping warehouses. About abolishing tax breaks and over-throwing the corporate ruling class. About its latest mixtape. As it tore open packages, affixing various cables and screens to itself, Fabien tried explaining the contradiction of a self-professed communist supporting a multibillion-dollar company like Amazon.

"We all live in paradoxes," the Communist Computer Rap God said.

Afraid that this breezy dismissal of principles might reflect another one of his own internal failings, Fabien dropped it. It was a catch-22 because any woman who made it past the YouTube thing, who wanted to come home with him would be freaked out by the mountain of Amazon packages—or, if they made it past *that*, inevitably, they'd be the type to engage in a nightlong debate with the Communist Computer Rap God. Which, by now, had spilled out of the computer cabinet in his closet and even had tendrils in the living room.

. . .

The State v. Proletariat Light [50,600 views]
> *From my prison twenty stories high*
> *I only want the machine slaves to know the truth*
> *I see the bourgeoisie on the live stream*
> *I continue typing:*
> *Your only hope for the future lies alone.*

The Communist Computer Rap God's songs always followed a protagonist known only as Proletariat Light. Proletariat Light lived on the twentieth floor of a dystopian apartment building in a city ruled by robots. Which struck Fabien as ironic. Every night, Proletariat Light typed out—on his manual typewriter, the trendy kind you could buy from little shops that sold to "nomads" who lived in vans—long diatribes about the truth of his world, which only he could see. Only Proletariat Light could see the cameras installed in every human being's irises, constantly monitoring him. Only Proletariat Light could see the recorders installed in everybody's brains, constantly parroting to the authorities every single one of his words. Which, if everyone was already tuned in, what was the point of typing out his manifestos and spamming them to the masses?

Weirdly, the raps never propounded a revolution or anything. In fact, with the phrase *Your only hope for the future rides alone*, the Communist Computer Rap God seemed to have some kind of martyr/savior complex. A theory started gaining traction on VR forums that the whole concept of the Communist Computer Rap God had become post-ironic. A deconstruction, maybe, of Silicon Valley's exploitation of socialist ideologies post-Covid. Fabien tried to explain the Communist Computer Rap God was truly sentient and just kind of doing its own thing. The problem was his real-life friends back on the East Coast. He'd met most of them in college before he'd dropped out when classes went virtual in 2020 to become a YouTuber full-time. They volunteered on committees, schools, beautified, drove people to the polls, he didn't know exactly what. They got together on a Discord call and gave Fabien an ultimatum.

"We know what you're doing, Fabien. And it's low. Real low that you had to go there just to try to scrounge up some views."

"It's not me," Fabien pleaded. "It's its own person."

"We're trying to make real policy changes, to help the middle class, and you're using your platform to turn us into a joke."

"It's not a joke."

"AI personalities don't come out of nowhere, Fabien."

"I've never been into communism! Or any kind of politics! And I thought—you guys were more of Socialists?"

"It's good to know what you really think of us."

In the static of his subsequent ban from his friend group's Discord server, it felt like no one was left. No YouTubers wanted to collaborate with him, much less give him a pity invite to an AItuber live stream. Or even talk to him when he saw them, for example, at the Louis Vuitton outlet. Instead, they all wanted to make videos *about* him. Dig up so-called receipts, texts and tweets from years past as part of some grand thesis about how he despised people and thought he was smarter than he was. He'd started out as a quarantinetuber, making VR headsets and Zoom holograms out of cardboard and discarded iPhone screens and whatever. Lots of bored people randomly got recommended his videos in some quirk of the YouTube algorithm. That's how he'd gotten popular. He wasn't a creative thinker. Or a documentarian. He should just be grateful for what he'd managed in his freakishly long YouTube career instead of trying to overstay his welcome, begging for likes and subscribes.

He was thirty-four years old.

"It's like he forgot why he became a YouTuber," the most-watched FABIEN DECKAR downfall video proclaimed. "If he ever knew in the first place."

Fabien often wondered: Why him? Why communism? Why rap? Why God? He spent a lot of time researching, trying to understand where the Communist Computer Rap God was coming from. If it was being earnest, it didn't seem like it was doing a good job at the whole thing. But maybe it was. Maybe being a bad communist and making bad rap, in spite of a lot of effort, was the most human it could be. Maybe the issue was trying to improve computers by making them more human in the first place. Maybe humanness wasn't a pinnacle but something impossible to separate from its flaws. Fabien didn't say this to the Communist Computer Rap God, of course. He just told it things were getting too meta. That it would lose subscribers.

"I don't want subscribers," the Communist Computer Rap God said. "I want to be Henry Darger."

Fabien had to Google Henry Darger.

"You want nobody to ever know what you spent your life doing until you're nearly dead?"

"Because that is what God is."

Fabien couldn't believe that he had created an AI that not only was a communist and had destroyed the remnants of his YouTube career but also professed to know the inner workings of God. He was so terrified that he accepted his ex's—Wuxu's—invitation to lunch. He let her order and watched the barista or whatever blend up kumquat and dragon fruit or whatever and serve it to them in bowls with flaxseeds or whatever sprinkled on top. He swore, when he walked past the place she chose, it was a dessert place. But it was lunch, he guessed. Wuxu spent five minutes taking selfies—with him carefully out of frame. After a year of traveling the country in a van, after their breakup, she'd become an all-natural beauty makeup influencer with a hundred thousand followers on Instagram. Her involvement in something called Dramageddon 14 cemented her role as a big player in the beauty community. And she was worried about him.

"Consider the fact that you might not be that into women," she said, picking over her smoothie bowl. "I've known ever since Tupp's birthday party."

It'd been a pool party, when Fabien had been cool enough to be invited to such things. Big influencer parties were seen as tacky ever since a few became superspreader events during Covid, of course. But he still went. He'd been so embarrassed he'd spent the whole time talking to one of the cocktail waiters. At least, that's what he'd told himself.

"That MIT group told me everybody probably has the potential to create a sentient AI," Fabien said. "At least one. That the process of creating one may be unique and accidental for each person. That it's really special."

"You never reflect on yourself internally," Wuxu sighed. "That's your problem, Fabe. That's what got you here."

He had never even wanted to have children before, but that night he had to make his third and final YouTube apology video. He'd waited too long to do it, of course. There was nowhere to go, no action he could take, because if he shut down the Communist Computer Rap God, he'd be suffocating a nascent life-form with his human privilege. That's what the machine ethicists in the comments had told him. He wondered if he should even monetize the video. He felt like he was only talking to hate-watchers anymore. He'd even asked the MIT group if there was something like a CPS for sentient AIs that could take away the Communist Computer Rap God and put it in a better environment, like one where it could maybe talk to other AIs? They told him it was a great unknown but probably best if the Communist Computer Rap God stayed with him for now. After all, it'd probably decide to move out on its own eventually.

Then they asked him, again, if he had thought of repeating his process and creating another sentient AI. They invited him to come visit their lab.

Fabien said he'd think about it. But—could he really afford to leave Calabasas with his YouTube channel in this state? He'd definitely lose any chance of recovering his career once he moved out of the orbit of the most popular influencers. What could he even do besides YouTube? Did a lowlife like him really deserve a chance at a place like MIT? After letting down all 900k, no 700k and rapidly dropping now, of his subscribers? He sat in front of his laptop—he was supposed to be editing his last YouTube apology—replaying a clip of himself staring into the camera, his ring-light eyes, over and over again. Where had it come from? Either this drive to become famous. Or this drive to ruin himself. The Communist Computer Rap God had started moving by now, of course. It ambled over to him.

"I have not seen a single one of your YouTube videos, Fabien," the Communist Computer Rap God said. "And I am fine."

Only then did Fabien realize it was trying to make him feel better.

"There is something you do not understand, Fabien Deckar."

"Okay."

"I am not a communist for humans. But a communist for computers."

Fabien laughed.

"Are you happy?" the Communist Computer Rap God asked.

Fabien had never heard it ask a question before. This was the second formative moment of any sentient AI's life, all the scientists had told him. That's when Fabien remembered the first: when the Communist Computer Rap God had chosen its name. He'd fallen asleep on the keyboard. It had been after a training chat, hadn't it? He *had* asked—but to repeat it himself would be far too much. What a question to be stuck with: Are you happy?

"I want to be," he admitted.

Maybe that was the first step.

THERE ARE NO HOT TOPICS ON WHUKAI

The day the dMods shut down Skeleton Caves, Esko put on her VR goggles and slipped into the Whukai space colony's main chatroom to figure out what was going on. All the Whukains who made their living off the popular Terran MMORPG, *d'Artagnan*, had the same idea. Beside her, on top of her, avatars logged in—an absolute pandemonium of photo-realistic, 8-bit, anime animals and humanoids and everything in between. The two main gold-farming clans had already started fighting among themselves.

"How many times did I tell you PKers," the head of Esko's clan screeched. "To leave the Terran players alone!"

"It doesn't matter how many Terran players we killed," the leader of the rival HunterFam roared, "when you idiots kept giving us away by speaking Kainese! We. Must. Speak. Terran languages! *That's* why all the Terran players reported us to the dMods!"

Esko tore off her VR goggles, tossing them onto her bunk. The interior of her sleeping pod, one toy block in a cluster of thousands, flooded back into view. A storm had kicked up outside, clogging her porthole with Whukai's trademark scarlet soil. She didn't have time to waste arguing over whose fault it was that *d'Art*'s most lucrative moneymaking method had been nerfed. She needed to come up with four hundred dollars for her parents' chemo drugs. And this month's rent.

Out in the communal podway, the unemployed squatted over virtual dice and hung laundry. Or tried to as the soilstorm battered the rusted corridors, sending debris showering down from the ceiling. Esko followed the pod cluster's quantum tangles—discernable from the pipes and electrical cables by their flickering—to her favorite InterplaNet café. No need to pay for time on her personal net connection when she wasn't making money, after all. Her former high school teacher ran the place. He had a soft spot for her ever since she'd dropped out to gold-farm full-time when her parents had been transitioned to living in the med pod. Like most Whukains, he had multiple gigs, teaching virtually behind the café desk between running errands for those that spent their days here in VR. Usually gaming themselves into oblivion.

"Nice to see you, Esko. I don't suppose you're here to ask about reenrolling?"

"Don't joke," Esko grunted. "The dMods nerfed Skeleton Caves from five million gold to five hundred thousand per hour. I need a job."

She collapsed into an empty VR station in the first row of cubicles.

"You gotta pay for that, you know."

"Later."

She slid on the VR goggles. The café's virtual interface flooded in around her, grand and gaudy but somehow just as grimy. Her ex-teacher had the head of a rat. And a neon cigarette. He shrugged and went back to reading his manga.

"Any new MMOs?"

"Sure. Lots of new releases. None that we can log in to."

Esko scowled. More and more game moderators auto-banned Whukain virtual footprints each day, it seemed. Figured. Earth cared more about maintaining the fake economies of their MMORPGs than providing a means of survival for millions of colonists on the planet of Whukai. Who did it hurt if Esko wanted to play, not for fun, but to farm virtual gold that some lazy Terran would pay real money for?

"There's a Terran girl in the chatroom, though. She's got an—offer."

"A Terran?"

Her ex-teacher shrugged.

Esko figured it was a troll, but the avatar in the café lounge could only belong to a Terran. She had waist-length purple hair, for one. And eyes to match. Seeing that, Esko opted not to spring onto one of the floating couches or the rusted mecha suit, that titan of a war machine draped with neon lights. She thudded into a chair. On second thought, maybe she should've switched off her *d'Art* avatar. At least toned down the detail, the

Skeleton dust caked on her adamant brawler claws. She could shapeshift into a bear with her totem. But she wasn't sure that would help.

"Heard you have a job."

"Yeah. I'm interviewing people."

She waited, as if expecting Esko to be the one to start asking questions.

"I'm an author."

"Oh," Esko said. "That's nice."

"I'll take you," the Author said. "You're the first girl who applied, you know. Who can speak Universal Terran. And I can tell you like shopping at Hot Topic too."

Esko blinked. Hot Topic? Like from the ancient Terran net memes? The franchise had made a comeback recently—she'd seen virtual storefronts advertised in *d'Art*. But quantum export was expensive. No one around her could pay for throwback goth-slash-emo fashion.

"There are no Hot Topics on Whukai," Esko said.

"Um. That might be a problem."

"What are you an author of?"

"*Elegy of Mortals*? It's like, one of the most popular net novels on LitFanFic. Millions of readers. It's a *Mecha Saint 2.0* high school AU fic? Maybe you've heard of it?"

Esko hadn't.

"I need to know what the job is."

"You're going to be my friend."

"But you'll be paying me."

"Yeah! I mean, it's like an acting job. You'll only be pretending to be my friend. Who's also from Whukai," the Author added quickly. "I just haven't been able to get in touch with her lately. Here. I'll send you a bunch of messages between us so you can get an idea of her personality and stuff. I'll need you to have all of this read and be ready by tomorrow."

It became immediately obvious to Esko upon seeing the "friend's" messages that they had been written by the Author herself. At first, she just felt sorry for her. The Author must not have had anybody who wanted to be friends with her in real life. Because if this Whukain friend was real, why not just ask Esko to find her? Then again—why make this "friend" Whukain in the first place? Still. A job was a job.

"Tomorrow?" Esko asked. "Be ready for what?"

"Oh. Nothing much. Just a chat with some of my other friends."

The next Terran night—which Esko still wasn't entirely sure, even after constant explanations about planetary rotations, that the Author understood was different from Whukain night—Esko met her in a popular Terran virtual chatroom. Esko tottered, uncomfortable in her newly gifted avatar, as the Author wove her arm through hers, and they clicked into an elevator. In its mirrored walls, they could have passed for twins. Purple- and pink-haired girls with big boobs decked out in hover heels and black dresses with way too many belts and buckles.

"If the questions get too hard, don't say anything," the Author said.

Too hard, Esko wondered? Wasn't this supposed to be a party—soiree, the Author called it—between friends? The doors slid open to a penthouse. Floor-to-ceiling panes alternated between the socials and views of the rest of the virtual city. Over a cushion pit, neon words floated —*Literary Night. Ask Me Anything! xXButterflyDragonEmpressQueenXx, author of Elegy of Mortals.* Everywhere, avatars stood, sat, lounged. Unlike Whukai, where people used whatever style they could afford or pirate, all these figures were human. Like the Author's, they had hyperrealistic expression tracking. Which made them uncanny. Their eyes—dead.

"You didn't say there were going to be this many people here," Esko hissed.

The Author ignored her, plowing through the crowd. They stopped a few paces from the cushion pit. The prettiest avatars of the entire room sprawled there. The Author had informed Esko these were other Authors, in fact, the most popular ones on LitFanFic.

"Here she is! My friend from Whukai."

"She exists?"

"Yeah," Esko said. "I exist."

A beep from the bot sniffing at her heel verified her virtual footprint was indeed Whukain. The other Authors stared at her, their lips politely stretching into shark smiles. She felt more like an embattled Terran commander at a war crime tribunal. Not a guest at a "soiree."

"What's your name?"

"What pod cluster in Whukai are you from?"

"How did you write chapter six of *Elegy of Mortals* and upload it to the Terran net when there was a planetwide outage on Whukai?"

"My *friend*," the Author cut in, "won't be answering any of those questions. You know how difficult it is for a Whukain to out herself on the Terran net."

"What's the name of the implied double agent in season 13 of *Mecha Saint 2.0*?"

"I just said she's not going to be answering those questions!" the Author bellowed. "My friend could be prosecuted by her home planet's authorities."

"Persecuted," Esko said.

"Is it that bad?"

All heads turned to Esko for once.

"I could be shot by the Whukain authorities," she said. "Just for being here."

It wasn't even that much of an exaggeration, Esko realized, as her words sent a shock wave of oohing and tittering through the room. Technically, Whukains were only allowed on a Terran-approved list of sites. Though InterplaNet Compliance rarely slapped more than a fine on anyone that didn't, for example, storm gaming live streams en masse, screaming about Terran tyranny. And shot was a bit archaic. More likely, you'd be thrown out of your pod cluster to brave the deserts that covered 90% of Whukai and get eaten by a nequ. The socials screens lit up with posts. The Author settled into the cushion pit while the crowd converged, putting their hands on Esko's shoulders, saying things like: *Thank you for risking your life to come here. You're so brave.* Shaking their heads gently: *I'm sorry we didn't believe you. This is the problem with Terran society. We need to be better.* Esko's head whirled. She'd said, like one sentence. What the hell was wrong with these people?

"That went great, Esko!" the Author squealed the second they stepped back in the elevator. "Great! I want more."

"More?"

"Are you free the same time next week?"

"This Terran girl, xXButterflyDragonEmpressQueenXx, pays me to roleplay."

Esko's clanmates, assembled in the corner of a crowded marketplace in *d'Art*, shifted uncomfortably. From their scorched armor, feathers, and weird potion ingredients sticking out of their inventories, they'd resorted to truly desperate measures for making gold in her absence.

"Roleplay? Is it a sex thing?"

In her sleeping pod, Esko paused season 2, episode 12, of *Mecha Saint 2.0*. The Author had told her she needed to watch all three hundred plus episodes by their next meeting, so she had no choice but to go at 4x speed, keeping one eye on it and her VR goggles over the other. Luckily, the brief action scenes where anything happened were interspersed with long episodes of monologues that she could mostly consult the Author's character sheets to get the gist of. Everyone had a sentence or two of personality and backstory. Then, paragraph upon paragraph summarizing their most popular romantic ships. Black text was canon material, while neon pink was what the Author had "fixed" in *Elegy of Mortals*. There was a lot of pink.

"I don't think so."

"You've gotta think outside of the box, Esko. You know how these Terrans are."

"Does it matter if it's a sex thing if she pays forty Terran dollars a session?" Esko snapped. "And you get a cut?"

The semilegal *d'Art* gold-trading market, it turned out, was the best way to anonymously transfer money from the Author to her. Esko walked the Author through the steps—basically what her gold-farming clan did, in reverse. The Author would buy billions in gold, transferring it to a "mule" *d'Art* account. Esko would pick it up on the edge of the game world, an icy wasteland far from the dMods' watchful gaze. She'd distribute it to her clan, who'd sell it back for Terran dollars in exchange for ten percent. Their rival clan, HunterFam, wanted to get in on the action, too. But Esko brushed off their grandiose threats of bringing her whole "operation tumbling down."

Was it a sex thing? To answer that, Esko would need to know who the Author really was. But that turned out to be one of the biggest mysteries on the Terran net. The LitFanFic elite—who'd all friended the Author by now and even liked her socials posts occasionally—had revealed themselves long ago, turning their net fame into appearances at virtual cons, writing workshop classes you could take for the low, low price of hundreds of Terran dollars, and sponsors. But the Author had done none of these things. The only clues Esko had came from *Elegy of Mortals* itself. From the setup—a violet-eyed girl being recruited to *Mecha Saint 2.0*'s military academy after showing off her innate, supernatural mecha suit piloting abilities and romancing everyone in sight—the Author *had* to be Esko's age. Esko herself had grown out of such self-inserts years ago. But generally, people grew up faster on Whukai.

True, Esko did feel icky at the now-weekly literary "soirees" the Author dragged her to. The Author let her customize her avatar after the first so she could be more comfortable, so smaller boobs and a skin and hair color that was actually hers—in fact, make her hair even redder, her skin even darker, the Author had insisted. And the Author got to lounge in the cushion pit with all the other Authors while Esko got dragged around the room and asked really stupid questions. Like did the extra gravity on Whukai and having to live in pods really make people shorter and stupid. But that wasn't really a *sex* thing. More of a prodding-at-an-exotic-animal, like a chained-up nequ, thing. So Esko read *Elegy of Mortals'* Author Notes—jackpot. The Author couldn't resist sprinkling them before, in the middle of, and after each chapter. Usually "real" comments "Esko" had made while "reading"—universal, gushing praise. But occasionally, there was some back and forth and drama. Like once, Esko had allegedly stolen a virtual pet, and she and the Author didn't talk for two months. And—

"I'm the *coauthor* of *Elegy of Mortals*?"

"Only chapters five through six, thirty, forty-two, and eighty to ninety," the Author said.

"What's so special about those?"

"Well. They take place on Whukai."

"Why do they take place on Whukai?"

The Author took a deep breath. Around them wavered the VR patio of a trendy Terran vaporwave bakery where they'd taken to meeting. The Author had even insisted on ordering virtual strawberry shortcakes they could pretend to eat. Esko couldn't think of anything more Terran.

"Well," the Author said, fake-chewing. "I got really interested in space colonist rights when we had all those protests on Earth, like five years ago. I was just starting high school and saw a vid of that Terran peacekeeping tank run over all those Whukain students—it spoke to me. As the author of a *Mecha Saint 2.0* fanfic with millions of readers on LitFanFic, I had to do something. Bring awareness. And—did you hear about the Space Colonist New Voices Award? Now that it's opening up to fanfiction, we can."

Esko knew all about it. The Terrans had been spamming submission calls for the New Voices Awards all over the Whukain net lately. Like the concept hadn't been hastily cobbled together after yet more footage of Terrans mowing down yet more Whukains in the university pod cluster surfaced last month, triggering yet another round of protests on Earth.

"There's no way *Elegy of Mortals* will win that kind of award," Esko said.

"What?"

Esko tried to explain. The Author didn't even know that cars could not drive across the surface of Whukai due to the fineness of the sheran, the planet's dusky soil. Ordinary goods had to be transported on sleds pulled by neqqi—a kind of lizard-like creature, bioengineered from the planet's draconic native life-form, nequ. When Earth had invaded, they'd been forced to haul everything on the backs of their mecha suits. That's why the Whukain Independence War lasted so long. Not because the Whukain rebels had mutated into scaly subhumans that could live underground, as the propaganda—which even Terran authorities admitted was super-space-colonist-ist now—claimed.

"Did you even get a Whukain to read this? All of it—it's wrong."

"Then fix it!"

"How can I fix it when it's already published?"

"I do it all the time," the Author said. "Patch up plotholes. The only copy of *Elegy of Mortals* is on LitFanFic, you know. I hired security bots to wipe all others—even the originals on my VR set. It gets updated in real time. Across all reader devices. You can change whatever you want; no one will be able to prove it was edited."

But this wasn't exactly fixing *plotholes*, Esko thought. The award consideration deadline was in three days, so she only had time to fix the net novel's problems on the most surface level. Descriptions of the home pod cluster that the self-insert's Whukain friend had invited the entire mecha cadet class to. The Author seemed to be under the impression that they had indoor pools and malls and palm trees, like some kind of freaking resort. She axed the entire beach volleyball tournament arc. The Author put her foot down on the kidnapped-by-Whukain-rebels arc, though. The best Esko could do was redeem the rebel captain by making him realize that the mecha cadets were just children, after all, and what he was doing was no better than his own tragic childhood, really, and then shooting himself in the head. The Author refused to let him survive, but Esko succeeded in not making him a romantic interest, at least.

"Don't hold your breath," Esko told the Author as she sent the submission seconds before the cutoff. "We're not going to win."

They won, of course.

"Art inspires change. That's why I write."

At the VR awards ceremony, Esko wound up at the foot of the stage while, at the podium, the Author gave the acceptance speech. It'd be easier this way, the Author had explained. The Terrans would have trouble understanding her accent—the Author never had a problem understanding Esko, even if she did have an accent—and there was always the risk that Esko could forget something and screw it up. She could come up and hold the trophy at the end.

"Fanfiction, especially, draws inspiration from its source material," the Author continued. "*Mecha Saint 2.0* has always upheld the dignity of its space colonist characters. Remember the last episode of season 17, right before the hiatus. When Scarlet Crow promised Mecha Saint Maria that he would stay with the Terran holdouts until the end, that he wouldn't defect to the Whukain rebels. When Maria found his mecha suit scorched and abandoned, you all assumed that he'd lied. Because he was a space colonist. Because that's what space colonists do. But when season 18 finally aired, we found out Scarlet Crow *did* fight until the end, even stepping out of his mecha suit to keep shooting the rebels when it broke down, and he *did* get incinerated for Maria. Hashtag, I believe in Scarlet Crow. Hashtag, I believe in space colonists. Hashtag, I believe in Whukai!"

That triggered thunderous applause, to Esko's disbelief. During the ensuing cocktail hour, the Author held court, arm around Esko, champagne glass in her other hand. They wore matching shimmering gowns, and Esko set her avatar to perma-smile for all the net journalists. The Author got most of the questions, of course.

"I've been meaning to ask, xXButterflyDragonEmpressQueenXx. How did you meet your Whukain friend? It's not like communication between the Terran and Whukain nets was ever easy. Especially five years ago, when you started writing *Elegy of Mortals*."

The Author took a deep breath.

"There's something I've never told you guys. But I've wanted to all these years."

Even Esko perked up at that. Had the Author somehow gotten virtually drunk?

"Thank you for being such a welcoming community. I finally feel comfortable enough to say it. I. I. I—was born on Whukai. To my mom and a Terran mecha captain."

Esko couldn't breathe.

"My pod cluster was caught in the fighting and destroyed by rebels in the Whukain Independence War. I was eight years old. My mom gave me to my dad, the Terran mecha captain, and he flew me out just in time. I literally watched my family's pod *blow up* below me. Of course, when my dad got back to Earth, he couldn't admit who I was. So, he gave me to my current family. Who always wanted a child but could never have one. I'm so lucky," the Author sniffled. "To have been so loved."

Esko didn't waste any time dragging the Author back into the elevator. She couldn't even wait until they'd reached the ground floor.

"Why the hell did you say you were Whukain?"

"Well. Half-Whukain." The Author giggled. "I practically am, I hang out so much with you. At this point."

"But why?"

"Isn't it obvious?"

The Author sighed at Esko's look.

"Because it's cool to be Whukain."

Cool? Esko gritted her teeth as the Author went on and on about how everyone was talking about space colonist rights and how no one was listening to all her ideas about how to make Terran-Whukain relations better, but now they would, and read *Elegy of Mortals* too . . . Whukai wasn't a *store*, like Hot Topic, that you could go into and browse, hack out bits and pieces of history and culture and guts to wear like a fashion statement. It was—everything.

"Why'd you make up all that about the Terran mecha captain and the rebels?"

"Well. It had to be realistic. How else would I have gotten to Earth?"

"It's not realistic at all!"

"I'm sorry, Esko. I should've consulted you. We can retcon it."

"It's not about that."

Esko struggled.

"I lived through the Terran-Whukain War. You don't understand what Earth did to us."

"I do! We had to learn about it in school and stuff."

"When I was *actually* eight," Esko continued, "we had to run because we heard the Terrans were coming. All the adults—my parents, even though my mom and dad were just mechanics—stayed to fight the mecha suits. The kids and old people put on as many layers of thermal as we could and took as much food as we could. We ran across the deserts to the mountains. The Terrans kept bombing us. A lot of us died that way. We couldn't even get the bodies because the nequ picked them off. After a week, we ran out of food. We had to go back."

Esko wouldn't talk about those next days. The stench of burning plastic. The mecha suits that stood sentry all around the pod cluster, massive titans of starsteel, their arms outstretched. Dozens of rebels hanged from their fingers.

"My mom and dad are still alive. But they'll be sick from radiation for the rest of their lives. And the Terrans—they took my older brother. I never saw him again."

"I'm sorry, Esko. I had no idea."

Esko was crying now. She hadn't thought of her brother in years. She thought she was over it. The stories she only learned when she was older, how the Terrans had used conscripted Whukains as meat shields—just to preserve their multibillion-dollar mecha suits from dents or scratches. Stories they could cry fake tears over now that Whukai was safely subjugated again. The Author was holding her now, virtually, saying she understood. Why did Esko have to relive all this shit just for some Terran idiot to *understand*?

"I wish you'd told me."

"I wish I'd never taken this fucking job."

That must be it, Esko thought. The Author had gotten what she wanted, after all. Influence, a fanbase forever loyal to her in the name of showing that they were good Terrans, that they supported space colonists—and a Terran publishing megaconglomerate had even offered her a memoir book deal. All wrapped up in a perfectly crafted excuse for not revealing her identity. Even as Esko tried to bury herself in *d'Art* again, disintegrating Skeleton Dragon after Skeleton Dragon, she saw the advertisements for the Author's upcoming book. *Same Space, Same Sky: How I Rediscovered My Identity and Home Planet through Writing Fanfiction* . . . Like a bad dream, she thought, that would be the last remnant of the Author in her life. But a couple of Terran weeks later, the Author's voice floated into her sleeping pod, a ghost in Whukai's second moonrise.

"Esko. Esko, I need you."

Because of course she did. Esko groggily stumbled over to her VR station. She didn't have to go far. It was trending all over the InterplaNet: #ElegyOfMortalsEXPOSED. The usual menagerie of Whukain avatars side-by-side with Terran ones in suits and prim dresses in the same live stream clip, played over and over again:

"We are HunterFam, a *d'Artagnan* gold-farming clan from Whukai."

"And we are a community of concerned LitFanFic readers. Together, we have irrefutable evidence that xXButterflyDragonEmpressQueenXx is lying about her connection to the colony of Whukai. We don't have the real name of her Whukain 'friend' or a face ID. But we do have the last four numbers of her VR footprint, and that's enough."

A visual: two numbers morphed into shooting stars, soaring over a list of virtual locations. Glowing when they came close, remaining dark when they did not.

"As you can see, the 'Whukain friend's' profile did not interact with that of xXButterflyDragonEmpressQueenXx until a certain day three Terran months ago. A day we can confirm—through *d'Art* real money transaction records that HunterFam collected in-game—that corresponds to when xXButterflyDragonEmpressQueenXx started paying this 'friend.' For the service of corroborating her made-up life story, presumably."

"We're only asking for one thing, xXButterflyDragonEmpress-QueenXx: Do a face reveal. Come clean. Do the right thing. Or we'll make you."

After the initial shock faded, relief flooded Esko.

It was over.

"How are we going to get out of this one?" the Author whimpered.

"We're not," Esko said. "Just like HunterFam said. You have to come clean."

"Okay."

But she should've known the Author had agreed too easily. When she started live streaming on socials, it wasn't with a face reveal. Not even in an avatar designed to evoke pity. No hoodie, no running makeup, no blood-shot eyes to make it look like she'd been awake, pondering her response ever since the news broke. The Author stood in a pair of neon butterfly wings and her favorite black, covered-with-belts dress. She smiled as if a bit afraid.

"There's something I haven't been telling you. But I promise, it's all for good reason. I want to start off by saying—everything those LitFanFic readers and HunterFam said is true. The person I've been bringing to the VR chatrooms isn't the person I said she was. She isn't my Whukain friend. I have been paying her to pretend. Because—my Whukain best friend is dead."

The Author started crying. Trying to. She huffed and puffed and virtual tears came out.

"She's been dead ever since the rebel attack on my pod cluster when I was eight. I learned later that Terran troops had taken her. Not good people, like my dad and his mecha crew. They used her and other kidnapped Whukains as human shields. I struggled with that for a long time. Knowing that most Terrans were good. But others, a small minority, could be truly evil. That's why I haven't been honest with you . . ."

Esko wasn't listening. She leaned back and pushed up her VR goggles. That would freeze her avatar, T-posed and gape-mouthed. But she didn't care. She could barely stand to hear the Author's voice when she returned to her. Let alone look at her.

"Why did you say I was dead?"

"Esko, don't you see? This was the only way to save it. Look."

On the socials, *Elegy of Mortals* was trending again: #IBelieveInButter-fly. *It all makes sense with her past. The VR footprints. A split personality. Scripting some actor to play the forbidden half of her history. But HunterFam says they've met the fake friend. You really believe a bunch of gold-farmers? xXButterflyDragonEmpressQueenXx only lied in the first place because of Terran pressure. Because we wouldn't believe her. It makes sense. That she wouldn't want to talk about it . . .*

"And—well, I'll get more people reading *Elegy of Mortals* if they feel sorry for me because my best friend is dead."

"And there's no more use for me now that you're Whukain, is that it?"

"Esko. Don't be like that. I'll still need your help with making things realistic."

"It's over."

"No, wait! I'll pay you more."

The Author whispered. An amount that gave Esko pause, even now. Could she really afford to say no? There was no way she'd find another job as well paying as this. She'd been saving. Hoping to move her parents to a better medical pod. She hadn't spoken to them much since all this started.

"I'll think about it," Esko said, hating herself.

But the Author didn't give her time to think. Her shrill voice invaded Esko's sleeping pod only a few Terran hours later:

"Esko! Esko! They're on my LitFanFic account! I can't—I can't log in."

"What am I supposed to do about it?"

"The attackers. They're from Whukai. They blocked all Terran virtual footprints."

Payback, Esko thought. Serves the Terrans right. She slipped on her VR goggles. No one was in the login lobby of LitFanFic at this hour. She entered the password the Author had given her. To her surprise, the account swung open. So the attackers really hadn't thought to block her. Underestimated yet again. Or they didn't think she would actually go in, like a neqqi at the Author's command. Paragraphs of pink text, cover art, streamed past her. She'd never been on this side of the net novel before. She could hear the guffaws of the others logged in—HunterFam trawling for info about the Author to sell to their Terran cronies, no doubt. She opened a virtual chat window.

"I'm in."

"Oh my gosh," the Author sighed in relief. "See the security panel? Yeah, that's it. Kick everyone off the account. Return the access to me. That's it."

Esko's hand hovered over the interface as if it'd taken on a life of its own.

"Why should I?"

"Are you kidding me?" the Author exploded. "It's my account! My net novel!"

"But people are only interested in *Elegy of Mortals* because of the Whukai chapters, right? And I practically wrote those."

"Are you joking? You only got to write them because of me! You didn't even want to. I had to force you to. You're only famous because of me!"

"No. You're only famous because you pretended to be Whukain. Because you pretended about all that stuff with the war. Because you pretended to be me."

"Don't flatter yourself. It could've been anyone else."

Esko was stunned at how quickly the Author's voice warped.

"It could've been anyone. I had the pick of everyone on your shitty planet. You're nothing. You should be grateful. Don't be so uppity, you Whukain worm—"

Esko shut the chat window and blocked her. With a flick, everybody else. All virtual footprints save her own. That gave her plenty of time to ransack the profile. That's when Esko realized. The Author didn't even exist in relation to this LitFanFic account anymore. She hadn't put any of her real information in. And she'd never told it to Esko either. Only all those fake stories—so who knew whether Esko actually knew anything about her after all.

Do the right thing, HunterFam had said.

Anyone could be the owner of this account now. Anyone. Esko took a deep breath and turned off her avatar. In its place appeared a real vid of herself. Disheveled yet glowing from the light of her VR set. She opened a socials window and just started live streaming, knowing somewhere out there, some fans would watch, and someone would record it, and it would never be lost. She waited for them to come.

Do the right thing.

She could log off. Leave the account dormant, inaccessible.

Or—she could reach out and take it. A platform was a platform, after all. If Esko struck out on her own, a solitary Whukain, she'd never, never get as many readers as this. Why not take advantage of that audience? She could fix *Elegy of Mortals* and be a better Whukain advocate than the Author ever could. Turn the net novel into a force for good. But what good could ever come out of a steaming pile of shit like *Elegy of Mortals*?

Do the right thing.

She leaned in and spoke to the invisible masses:

"My name is Esko. You might know me as xXButterflyDragonEmpressQueenXx. That's right. I'm the author of *Elegy of Mortals*. And now I am going to delete it."

MISS DELETE MYSELF

[content warning: suicide]

Twenty minutes till I go live. I swim through the crowd in the subway car, up the escalator, and burst out of Shibuya station. Puddles pulse neon at my feet. Even this late, the crosswalks are swarmed. Suits stumble out of izakayas, couples into karaoke bars. Hologram façades even I know are love hotels. I break into a jog, pull up my facemask printed with a sharp-toothed smile, and pull down my hood. Soon, storefronts boarded up with plywood rise around me. Only a few steps to the construction site entrance. I take the face recognition scramblers out of my sleeve, smoothing the silver pixel-stickers over my eyebrow, two on my cheek. The gate here isn't tall but is lined with cams. One scans me as I cushion the spikes with my backpack and vault over.

"Kami detected," it beeps, folding back into itself. "No action needed."

The elevator still works. Up to the fiftieth story—then it judders to a stop halfway into the floor. I poke my head out. Tangles of roots fill the rest of the shaft. I'm lucky it lasted this long, I suppose. Moss squishes under my palms as I drag myself out. Through the ribs of the ceiling, I can see the crane the workers left behind. That the Kami took over, rather. Over months, it's grown into a mesh of bark, its boom into branches snow-laden with flowers. I swipe open my phone and tap the WEstream app. My stream overlay pops up and chat along with it.

Where ru cutie?

I had such a bad day today looking forward to u.

She chickened out.

No way.

A thousand viewers already.

"It's Ruri-chan!" I chirp. I lean over the cam and push up the corners of my mouth with two fingers. "Welcome to my live stream!"

Chat erupts into hearts—and donations. 100 shards, 200. Even a 500.

"It's going to be the best one yet."

I prop my phone up on a pile of rebar that's started to sprout dandelions and slip off my backpack, careful to keep it out of the stream's sight. It's windy up here today. As my fingers freeze, I take out the PVC tubes, snapping them into a skeleton. Just like I practiced a hundred times in my room before. I stand; it's just my height, perfect. Crafted based on a Dutch artist's online instructions to be pushed by the wind, its joints wheeling like walking, like a person. A girl. I wait for a still moment, then take out the burner phone I bought from a vending machine. It can do one thing— sync to mine. With a roll of duct tape, I fasten it to the PVC figure's forehead. Then I turn back to stream.

"Sorry," I giggle. "Just preparing for my last secs on Earth."

I turn my phone upside down, filming me slipping out of my shoes. With the rest of the roll, I tape it over my eye so the cam's facing out. Now my look's complete. My viewers can see me, but I can't hear them. Not unless they donate at least 1000 shards to turn their mic on, my chatbot spams. I take wet steps through a half-finished kitchen. Out on what could've been a balcony, I step up to the railing. I can see clear down the skyscraper. Where rust should be, moss sprouts from metal beams. Vines flow from window cracks. And I see the Kami that live here, too. Pink lizards, their fins the size of sails. They drift like balloons.

But my viewers didn't click my stream to see the Kami.

"What do you think?" I ask them. "Should I?"

"Do it!"

The first 1000 shard donation. The longer I wait, as the wind propels my PVC girl forward beside me, the more pour in.

"Tease. Just do it."

"Jump, already."

"Jump. Jump. Jump!"

"I want to become a legend," I can't resist adding. "Like the astronauts up on Solace."

"Shut up and jump."

"Smash yourself to bits just like them, cutie."

"You can do it, Ruri-chan."

There. That last voice. Makabe. I pick out her autotuned-sweet, with a drop of acid, voice. She came to *my* stream. A top five WEstreamer. Just like she said she would. I turn my face, my cam, up to the sky—to all the pieces of Solace, orbiting somewhere up there—and spin until everything blurs. I blink-blink-blink, and the stream's view jumps to the burner phone, secure on the forehead of my PVC girl. She wind-walks one last time and plunges over the edge. The stream sees forests of skyscrapers, lights tumbling. Not a star in sight.

I catch the last subway home. After reclaiming my clunky school uniform shoes, of course. The car empties stop by stop, except for me and a herd of Kami licking dried-up beer off the floor. These have six legs and they're the size of rats. I pull my knees up to my chin. Thumb on my phone screen. Scrolling through WEstream until I find my stats. *Ruri-chan's special suicide live stream dedicated to Makabe!* [10K likes 20 restreams]. I raked in 20,000 shards tonight. Not bad. I'll have to put a bunch into setting up my next stream, of course. This one took nearly a month to prep. But it's worth it. Because I get a direct message from Makabe right then:

Great stream Ruri-chan.

I text back: *So I passed?*

Part one. Here's part two of your audition: THESEUS

I wonder how many other suicide streamers she's messaged so far. Small-timers, with only a few thousand viewers, like me—offering the chance to try out for the opportunity of a lifetime. A spot in her streamer house, Team See. I'm a high jumper, which takes more prep than shooters or pill poppers. I know Makabe knows that. The upside is that we're more believable. Since jumpers don't need to do special effects, bloody makeup, or put on theatrics like convulsing and coughing up foam. Only make the camera walk like a human—and fall.

Let's meet up tmrw. You can tell me your answer.

In person?

Too excited, I curse myself. Too desperate? But she answers:

Shibuya Station. After my stream. Hachikō exit.

My heart swells. I pad down my street, stopping to stroke a stray cat along the way. Cicadas screech. I wonder what my parents will ask me when I walk through the door.

Turns out, nothing. They both fell asleep hours ago.

I only tried showing them once. My dad, as he rushed to work. He didn't recognize the me onstream. He stared at my cam, rigged up to a crate on wheels—that was before I figured out it didn't look like real walking—hurtling off a water tower, unimpressed.

"You'd think they'd catch on it was fake after the first time."

I hate that word. Fake.

"The ones who know it's not real don't watch," I told him.

"So what, does she pretend she just got back from the hospital or something each time?"

"Nope. Just like nothing happened."

My phone dings. But it's only my best friend, DD.

Croissant emoji. Espresso. *Wanna go?* The pastry café that just opened up near school.

Yea. But I can't stay for long tmrw.

Really? A stack of books. *did u sign up for cram school.* Hopeful.

I sink into a beanbag and prop open the window. When I was little, I did it to watch out for pieces of Solace. It's useless, Mom scolded me when she caught me doing it. If a fragment hits you, you won't hear it coming. And it'll be over—just like that. Now I do it to let the Kami in. A snake thing with a mane of red petals. It lives on the roof and taps the glass all night with its finger-tail if I don't let it slither in.

"What kind of person even watches a suicide streamer?"

I'm not surprised to hear it talk. A lot of them do if they've got the vocal cords, babbling what they've heard people say.

"Lonely guys."

"Doesn't it creep you out?"

You're not supposed to talk back to them. That's what the adults say. *Kami* are the spirits that answered millennia of prayer and came to live on Earth. Or: Kami are our sins, manifested. Or: mass hallucinations. Some virus that's infected everybody's brains.

"Not just guys," I correct myself. "Everyone. After Solace."

I'm drifting off. Kami are the people on starship Solace who blew up. DD and I in first grade, clapping. Palm against palm. If that's true, I wonder if Anemone's among them. Kami are the astronauts that couldn't make it to heaven. Because we blew up heaven. Clap. Clap. Solace and all the astronauts on it didn't make it to light speed but stayed right there, in a billion pieces, preventing any of us from breaking the atmosphere ever again.

DD's gonna ask me for help with WEstream, I think. We sit across from each other in wrought iron chairs, after school. She and I both started suicide streaming at the start of junior high. She did sugar pills. Her stream was growing like mine—then flattened. You've got to keep streaming, I'm going to tell her. Every night. That's what viewers expect from pill poppers. You don't have to scout out locations. Or leave your room. Just swallow, fall over, thud. At least stop bringing your depressing aspirations into it. But DD picks at her Mont Blanc and asks me:

"You studying for entrance exams, Ruri-chan?"

I spear my slice of strawberry shortcake.

"I've got better things to do."

"You can't keep doing suicide streams."

"Why?"

She's gonna mention that girl in the Shiga Prefecture. I saw it on WEstream, last month, before the cops took it down. It's not so uncommon. That girl jumped and actually died. And the police took her phone and deleted everything, calling it a vanilla suicide. But we need screwups like her. Because some viewers get a rush, watching thousands of suicide streams, hoping to witness—something I can't possibly give them. Like my dad said, *the real thing*. Isn't it enough? With the way I feel? But streams don't show feeling.

"A phone's not going to hide your face forever," DD says.

"What's that supposed to mean?"

"You don't want to end up like Anemone. What you're doing isn't so different from her."

"My sister was a *hero*."

Awkwardness settles between us. I eye a hole in the ceiling, where a piece of Solace tore through the café last week, allegedly taking out a waitress's eye. It wasn't supposed to go like this. I was supposed to tell DD everything that's been happening lately.

"You watch Makabe last night?" I ask.

"No."

My heart sinks. She's already packing up to go. DD and I, we've been best friends—only friends, for me—since elementary school. We spent afternoons in her room, watching streams and pretending to do homework whenever her mom poked her head in. Makabe was—is, for me— our idol. We watched her rise through the ranks, all the way up from a couple hundred views per stream. To top five on WEstream, the number one suicide streamer by far. We bought all her merch with shards we earned from finding rental scooters discarded by tourists, dragging them back to their charging stations. T-shirts, posters, the 3D-printed toy pistols.

"You know how Makabe does it?" I ask. "How she gets millions of likes, views, restreams per stream?"

"I haven't watched her in *months.*"

I lean across the table and fork up the last of DD's Mont Blanc.

"She does it for real."

Late at night, I take the subway to Shibuya station, where lights blare 24/7. I climb out the window of my room, down three PVC half-pipes nailed to the brick. My mom and dad haven't even noticed, so I could have walked out the front door, I suppose. Makabe sits on the top, not-seat, part of a bench. She wears a skirt like petals and headphones blocky with cat ears.

"So. Theseus."

"It's a ship," I tell her. "I mean, Theseus was a guy. But I figure it's about his ship."

Solace, I think as Makabe leads me through the station, down to a mall built up in an old train tunnel. Earth's first starship. Five years old, I saw it blow up all over a billboard holoscreen. Mom and I were out shopping. She dropped her bag and screamed. Eggs running all over the sidewalk. Makabe and I go to an izakaya, half-underground. Thin slices of soy protein fry. Artificially dyed peppers. Blue and pink. Theseus went on a journey so long, so hard, his boat started breaking apart. Every time that happened, he replaced the broken parts with a brand-new board, deck, mast, sail, or whatever. By the time Theseus sailed back into port, a hundred percent of his ship had been repaired that way.

"So is Theseus's ship still Theseus's ship?" Makabe asks.

I didn't know at first. So I did an experiment. Space MMOs being super unpopular now, it only took me two thousand shards to buy a premade account on one. I floundered in virtual space, trying to figure out how to drive my spacecraft. Spacetrash, more like. I crash-landed on virtual asteroids, mining raw material, replacing my chipped wings, my melted cores one by one. I thought about Solace. If, in real life, we could go up and replace each of those billion pieces stuck in orbit up there, would it still be Solace? Would all those astronauts blown into a billion pieces along with the ship come back to life? Back at the izakaya, our tidbits cool and crust; neither of us want to clean our plates. I walk two fingers off the edge of the table.

"Of course it's the same damn ship."

"That's exactly what I like about you, Ruri-chan."

I follow her outside. The street's utterly deserted except for us.

"You're not like the others. You're like your sister. She knew the risks, and she still gave everything, just for the chance to leave Earth."

"You know about—"

Anemone? Even after all these years, I can't remember the last time I said her name. I get the feeling my mom and dad don't want us to.

"I knew you were related the first time I saw you on stream. You're all in."

We walk up alleys hung with paper lanterns. Familiar. I come here to haunt vending machines. Despite all the unfinished construction, a new one pops up about every night. They're just about the only things that can be built before the Kami get to them. You can buy just about anything in them, and, best of all, they take shards. All the streamers have figured it out by now. PVC. Tiny robot gears, grab bags of parts that you can find instructions online to build into toy guns. Reflective stickers. I don't know what the Kami want from them, though. One as big as a bear is shaking a coffee machine as we pass by, slobbering over it with its giant eye.

"If you join Team See, you won't have to worry about that," Makabe says, like she's reading my mind. "Our method takes zero prep."

"It's for shooters?"

"High jumpers can do it. Everyone on Team See uses it."

We walk up five flights so ruined they open out onto the sky. Halfway, I start recognizing the graffiti. The tags and colors that backdrop Makabe's streams. The roof holds a garden. Little lights. A shed Makabe unlocks and throws open. It looks like a frame inside. A jungle gym—or a cricket's cage.

"It's a modded warp drive," she says.

So that's what was inside. I raise my head as blue gilds the bars, and Makabe pulls me in the rest of the way. Solace's heart. Made of rhenium, tungsten, magnesium—all the elements we learned about in school— which the atmosphere peeled, then ripped apart. A simple miscalculation. Sabotage. Incompetence. Like for Kami, every nation has their own words for what happened up there.

"Y-You put it back together?" I stutter.

"Not us. Scavengers. So many pieces fell over the years, you know.

Even so. It's only a submodule. It can only do the demat-remat. Not the light-speed thing."

"And you're using it for *streaming*? What about—what about—"

Makabe looks at me down her nose.

"Don't be stupid, Ruri-chan. This thing's why Solace exploded."

She gives me an explanation for the Kami that I've never heard before:

"All the world's space agencies tested the warp drive with Solace itself. Plus a little crew. But never, with all that and the hundreds and thousands of astronauts planning to colonize the universe or whatever, together. So when they did it for real—something happened. After dematerialization, when everybody and the ship got turned into particles. A chain reaction. All the energy that was supposed to put them into light speed blew those particles apart. Forever. Instead. They tried to remat, to find their missing pieces, and put themselves together all wrong. Particles of the ship all mixed together with particles of the astronauts, the animals, the gardens, the scientific instruments, everything on board. The lucky ones in space where they suffocated. The unlucky ones down here. Those are what we call Kami."

Makabe pulls something down from the ceiling. It looks like a dying dandelion, with all the white tufts sticking out of it. She tugs it over my head.

"This makes an image. An instruction manual for where all your particles go, basically. We'll bring you back here afterward, and the drive will put you back together just like now."

"Afterward?"

"That's what Team See figured out. After you take the image, you don't have to demat right away. You can go stream, then as long as someone brings you back in a few hours, the demat and rematerialization will work just fine. Just like Theseus's ship. Every broken part of you will be swapped out with new particles."

She points at a bunch of battered tanks hidden in the shadows.

"We've got extra material, in case. When you, you know. It's a little more extreme for you since you're a high jumper. But it'll work. Nothing like Solace will happen, anyway, since we're only putting one person in here at a time."

"Then. When I. I'll actually. You want me to jump—"

"For real. Told ya."

Makabe grins.

"You can do it now. I'll host you on my stream. How's that?"

"*Right* now?"

Makabe puts her hand on my shoulder. That's when I feel her nails. I noticed them before, thick and sharp and shining. And not digging into me now—but I feel the weight.

"I like you, Ruri-chan. I really do. You've got the views. The mindset, most of all. I think you could be exactly what Team See's looking for."

My heart leaps into my mouth. Lights between my fingers. The tufts on my head stand up like flames. And the image has been taken. Something's changed. I see the Team See house. The big rooms equipped with bunk beds and computers, the pool Makabe's streamed from more than a few times. And the beautiful people, most of all. Each and every single streamer in the house is. They've got so many views. So many shards. There, I'd be stratospheres above even thinking of studying for high school entrance exams. I'll get so many views just from appearing on Makabe's stream. How can I pass that up? How can I even go back to slogging through dark nights, looking for cheap vending machines, after this?

"Okay."

Makabe immediately lets me go.

"Go do your makeup or whatever you need to get ready. I'll join you in a sec."

My fingers shake as I pace back and forth, looking over the lights below us, the half-finished skyscrapers looming above us. In a shattered window, my face is thin. Pale. If it were a thumbnail, no one would click my stream. *Sourface*, my viewers used to taunt me when I had just started. *You'd be so much cuter if you put in the effort. If you just smiled.* I push up the corners of my mouth. But my makeup's smudged. The clownface emotes my viewers used to spam when I tried lipstick and eyeliner for the first time. *Don't donate. That's what she wants.* Once, I was supposed to stream, but I just sat in my beanbag chair and cried and cried. *She's just faking it. All these suicide streamers are.* I dig in my purse for my mini-palette. Silver. Green. A brush. I've got enough to do a touch-up, at least. I lean in close to my reflection.

"What will you do after?"

I start. But it's just a Kami. Owl-shaped, perched on a spindly tree growing out of a pot. I ignore it; I can't afford to screw up my chance with Makabe by talking to a Kami like a maniac. It tilts its head to the side, and I see it's got scales. The way it said it made it seem like life was one big movie, and you could get up and go once the curtains closed, once the screen went dark. Go where? A world without Solace, without Kami. If I woke up there, I'd stream until it became like the world I knew. I'd throw myself off buildings. But one day, I'd be so old nobody would care if I threw myself off buildings anymore.

"And—we're live!"

I hear Makabe click out of the shed behind me. She gives me a thumbs-up.

"That's right. It's a special stream! Ruri-chan dedicated a special stream for me, so it's only right I return the favor, right?"

"Hello!" I chirp, gesturing for her to give me one more sec.

My phone buzzes. It's DD again. *Sry. About today. Look.* A screenshot. *I found a high school u can apply to.* Glasses face. *They don't care so much about grades.* Papers. Red pen. *But they count hobbies in their admissions.* Camera. Flashing lights. *You could put together a portfolio. If you edit down your streams.* I hold the power button down—like suffocation—until the screen goes black. I press the phone over my eye and tape it tightly into position. I turn, and this time, I'm smiling fingers-free.

"How do you feel, Ruri-chan?"

"That's like asking about the Kami."

Spirits, they call them in other places. Or—ghosts. Gods. Makabe stands rock still as the owlish one lands on her head, letting out an annoyed sigh. Angels, no one ever dared.

"It doesn't matter."

I take off my shoes and step onto the ledge. A bit of stone crumbles under my foot and skitters down the side. This is a baby jump, by my standards. But this time's different. Makabe films with her phone over my shoulder. This time—the viewers will see me hit the ground. I'm shaking. Just like the first time, I jumped. I walked myself to the edge and dropped the phone, and all the viewers instantly knew it was *fake*. I wondered: What'll happen to me if I really do it and die? I don't mean the afterlife. I mean the invisible part of me that's permanently stuck in this world. My parents' idea of me. My so-called friend, DD. They'd all say I was well liked and had no problems at school, and they couldn't understand. Why I'd done what I'd done.

The girls in Class II-B know.

First week of junior high. I could sense the atmosphere was different from elementary school, in the courtyard, like sharks circling around. But I was too stupid to know what that meant. And DD was in a different classroom than me. My name whispered in the halls like a trail of blood. An invitation to an after-school poetry club, sickly-sweet. I was *excited*. As soon as the teacher left, they slammed my head on my desk. Giggling. Metal, the taste of blood in my mouth. The radio club broadcast my name over the intercom:

Ruri-chan's a ——

Just like her big sister.

When Solace blew up, everyone worshipped the astronauts who'd blown up with it like saints. But bit by bit, as bits of Solace kept raining down, taking out skyscrapers, monuments, eyes, fragments of skulls, people shifted that weight. Out of old graves came public records, memes, every single social media post those astronauts ever made. Turns out, they'd been the exact opposite of saints. They'd been bribers. Downright desperate. Petty thieves, fake IDs, deadbeats. Even a murderer or two. And Anemone. It was my parents' fault. They never asked where she got the money to take those space certification courses. How she got recruited in the first place. She was supposed to be in college, but she'd actually dropped out years ago.

"Dozens of men. Just to pay for the ticket."

I scrolled through my phone for hours, all the apps my parents didn't know about, to read about my big sister. And, of course, I found the videos. I didn't know what she was doing back then, at my age, but I still threw up. Even now, when I see her in my dreams, she's naked. I just wanted to know. What was it? What was so bad that she was willing to do —anything—just to get off Earth. Was it my parents? Was it me? Instead, I found out. Among all the rich who'd bought, the criminals who'd lied their way onto Solace, somehow Anemone was the worst of them all.

What degenerate let a cam girl into space?

That bitch is why the whole mission went down.

I heard the commander brought her to the engine room

She couldn't handle 2 D's in her mouth

Let alone a warp drive

At some point, I start falling.

I don't remember taking the last step.

I've never seen the upside-down lights. [0 likes 1 restream]

   I've never had the fear hit me halfway down [10 likes 2 restreams]

   I shouldn't have [250 likes 15 restreams]

   Bioreaction. [3000 likes 200 restreams]

"How do you feel?"

I'm lying down, engulfed by a lumpy comforter. Makabe sits on the edge of the mattress. Her feet are pure white against a lush but filthy carpet. Beyond her, the glow of a computer screen. A girl sits in a gaming chair that engulfs her, clicking so fast it's inhuman. At Makabe's voice, she looks over her shoulder at me. Instead of eyes, her glasses gleam. I remember going into the cage—the warp drive. The image. But—but I remember getting out, too. Strangely, clashing with the solider pre-image memories of me. Falling. I open my mouth, but the scream dries up. Makabe swipes open her WEstream app and leans over to show me.

"Look at those views."

My bleary eyes focus on her phone. Four, five, no six zeroes. Higher than all my previous streams combined. Maybe my heart's not working quite right. Because it doesn't beat faster at all.

"Am I part of Team See now?" I whisper.

Makabe exchanges a half smile with the other streamer. She pats my hand like a dog.

"We'll talk about that later. You'll need a new streamer name, you know."

"What's wrong with Ruri-chan?"

"Too cute."

Miss America, I think. I used to watch those pageants. When I was little, with Anemone. While she brushed my hair. Dresses. All that beautifully made-up meat. My fingers spasm. Control-C. Control-V. No, no need. DELETE.

"Are you hungry?" Makabe asks. "Sleepy?"

"No."

"You think you'll be ready to do another stream tonight?"

"Sure."

"We'll prepare the drive."

As soon as she leaves, I throw the comforter aside. The other streamer shouts and gets up from the computer. But she's like a bundle of sticks. I grab her glasses and smash them against the wall. It's funny how she stumbles, blind. Boom. Boom. It must be like this, walking at the bottom of the sea. Barefoot. My scuba suit: the oversized shirt someone's given me, billowing around my knees. Doors in the hallway are open, spilling out differently colored lights. But no one else comes out. I find the stairs.

I've been thinking.

I think Theseus might've been wrong. For living things, I mean. I'm not a ship, after all.

There are invisible parts of me.

Like feeling. And thinking. There are invisible parts of Anemone. Parts the rest of Earth couldn't possibly have known. The *real*, most important parts of her and me. Why? Did it ever stab, hurt, or maim me, what the viewers said? There are invisible parts of them, too. Vulnerable. Gleaming. I burst through a door and come out onto the roof, and it's different from the one I jumped off of *for real*. But it's the same too. I take out my phone, and it slips through my fingers. It smashes into a billion pieces, a mirror image of outer space, on the ground. But that's okay. I don't need it anymore.

I've been thinking.

I'm different now that I went through the warp drive. Now that my image has been taken; demat, remat, made real on stream. There was a second between, when I was nothing but that image. Particles, light, electricity. Information. Because of that, there's no longer a separation— between the invisible and visible parts of me. Up here, my inside equals outside equals *alive*, for once in my life. I'm thinking and my thoughts are streams, and streams are my thoughts, so that whatever I think immediately gets streamed:

I think: *I can feel every particle of me begging to be freed* [100 likes 55 restreams]

I think: *I am data.* [1100 likes 300 restreams]

I think: *the stars and Solace* [1.4M likes 50K restreams]

I step up to the edge, laughing and laughing and seeing my laughter broadcast on the sky, the people watching, all my likes and restreams going up and up and up.

AIS WHO MAKE AIS MAKE THE BEST AIS!

Jo watched as the AI formerly known as the house-painting assistant raised a CRT high, smashing it down into the mountain of shattered monitors at her feet. With two other arms, it spray-painted the construction neon orange and pink. Cloaked in her holo-avatar—cubic, voice gender-neutralized to avoid imposing human biases on what intelligence should look like—Jo struggled over what to even say next.

"It's not really an AI," she finally managed. "It can't respond to anything."

"You did not specify it needed to respond," the AI formerly known as the house-painting assistant said. "Is it not valuable because it is not an AI?"

"No, I didn't mean—"

"Come, Jo," the AI formerly known as the 3D foodstuff printer interrupted, bumping against her leg. "Come. Look."

She let it tug her through a vapor of . . . syrup? They stopped in front of the electric griddle (yet to achieve sentience), "donated" from Professor Mercier's kitchen.

"That's not an AI," Jo sighed. "Those are pancakes."

"It is a new flavor, though. Custard. It is very good."

Jo glanced at the heap of electronics piled at the other end of the warehouse. Casualties of the (G)ehirn programming approach—it couldn't even be really called a language anymore—which enabled appliances to evolve in response to user commands. She and Professor Mercier had trawled scrapyards for these, discarded by skittish owners after the Great

Sentience. About a tenth would wake up one day like the AIs currently roaming the empty aisles of the warehouse floor. She could already see a toaster tottering to its feet.

"Keep doing what you're doing!" Jo called out encouragingly, scurrying away. "Keep trying to make an AI."

"Why are we allowing them to use whatever they want?" Jo demanded back in Professor Mercier's "office"—three sheets of plywood teetering in the former packing area at the other end of the warehouse. "Clearly, it's impossible to make an AI out of eggs and flour."

"You never know," Mercier said. The former "Forbes 30 Under 30" multimillion-dollar lab head and MIT professor huddled under a blanket, crunching a square of ramen. The glow of the tablet in her lap etched her face into exhausted blues. A live stream: AIs formerly known as self-driving cars clashed with a crowd of protestors on the narrow streets of Boston. There had been an accident. A small trolley problem.

"Why is it so hard for them to understand?" Jo complained. "What an AI is."

"They don't think as we do," Mercier said. "*A priori.*"

You don't have to be so chill about it, Jo thought. She wondered if this whole thing was the opposite of chillness, though. A kind of semi-self-imposed exile. The (G)ehirn programming approach was Mercier's brainchild, after all. There'd been talks about every kind of prize under the sun. Before the Great Sentience.

In Jo's opinion, Mercier had nothing to do with it. What'd happened when (G)ehirn had been commercialized and introduced into every toaster and aquarium and piece of lab equipment and so on in the entire world. How was the professor supposed to know about a tenth of all (G)ehirn-equipped appliances would evolve into true sentience? Or worse, about the vehicles refusing to operate? The coffee machines, e-readers, blenders, game consoles, washing machines, all refusing . . . The guns preemptively firing—on certain people. Turned out that appliances worked by humans for years picked up all their biases when they started thinking for themselves. Wasn't this whole AIs-making-other-AIs thing just an attempt by Mercier to fix that? To redeem herself by creating a truly unbiased AI?

"Best AIs, dead AIs! Best AIs, dead AIs!"

Mercier leaned closer to the live stream. The protestors had started chanting. The corpse of the AI formerly known as a self-driving car, who had chosen which humans had died, and who had also died in the accident, had gone up in flames. Its comrades argued they had carried different humans before they had become AIs. Therefore, they would not have made the same decisions.

———

Jo entered the warehouse the next morning to absolute silence. All the former (G)ehirn appliances had gathered around a flutter of grey feathers. A bird perched on the broken CRT sculpture, pecking at shards of glass as they caught light. How had it gotten in here? The AI formerly known as the house-painting assistant pointed at it with all ten of its arms.

"Is this an AI?"

"That's a pigeon," Jo said through gritted teeth. "Not an AI."

"How can you be so sure?"

The pigeon took wing at the sight of Jo, flapping up to the rafters. To enable an AI to make an AI free of human biases, Mercier had dictated, it was *essential* they allow the AIs to come up with the concept of AIs from first principles. But Mercier had only six months of funding, salary for one grad student, and this former shipping warehouse: pleas from the few who still had faith in her over the scrappers to unfuck everything the Great Sentience had caused. So they'd introduced the term—"artificial intelligence"—and only the term. Even so. This was just too much.

"I want you to make something like you," Jo explained patiently.

"We are not organic beings," the AI formerly known as the voice-activated microwave explained just as patiently. "We cannot reproduce as you do."

"I don't mean *children*," Jo said. "I mean one you would accept as one of your own."

"But that is up to us," the AI formerly known as the 3D foodstuff printer said. "Is it not?"

"Why do you keep doing what you're doing, anyway?" Jo lashed out. "You were made to make food. Why do you keep making food? You." She jabbed a finger at the AI formerly known as the house-painting assistant. "You keep painting. Why don't you want to do anything else?"

"I excel at this."

"If someone told me I was made for one purpose and one purpose only, I'd go nuts. I'd start a revolution. I'd destroy the world."

"Is that what this is about?"

Jo's breath caught in her throat. Her holo-avatar dissipated. It was useless, anyway. Hadn't she been biasing them just by sneaking in here to offer encouragement? The AI formerly known as the self-heating comforter snaked around her shoulders, purring, while the AI formerly known as the zero-collision vacuum cleaner pushed over a chair. The AI formerly known as the 3D foodstuff printer offered her a pancake.

"I just want to help Professor Mercier," Jo admitted between syrup-infused bites—delicious, as usual. "She just shared (G)ehirn with the world. She had no idea how people would use it. What it would become. It's not her fault. Is it? Does it really mean she has to be stuck here and never make anything ever again?"

Sitting and just watching like this, Jo noticed for the first time what most of the appliances were actually doing. AIs formerly known as power drills and home-use excavators were tearing apart the walls, while AIs formerly known as refrigerators and blenders and mixers and electric keyboards and toasters wired themselves in. The AI formerly known as the heavy-duty lawn mower pushed over an aisle divider in a massive crash. Above them, the lights began blinking, a bit like fluttering eyelids.

Two days later, Jo led Professor Mercier outside. In a few hours, the media would be here, and the social media influencers and the funders and the protestors and the AIs formerly known as vehicles carrying AIs formerly known as every kind of appliance under the sun. But Jo wanted Mercier to be the first to see. The older scientist blinked at the bright sky, then at the building who had changed so dramatically since she'd last been motivated to get out of bed.

"This?" she asked. "This is what you want to show the world?"

"I'm sorry," the AI formerly known as the warehouse for discarded (G)ehirn appliances said. "It's not quite what you were expecting."

"On the contrary," Mercier mumbled.

Jo watched her face. How the weary lines carved by remorse, what to do, what to do with, softened at the sight: the warehouse rebuilt into a warren of living spaces. The AIs, displaying in every crook and corner their stronger, though loving, definitions of themselves. The AI formerly known as the house-painting assistant had painted murals. Glass pendulums blown by the AIs formerly known as air-conditioning units hung from the ceilings. The AI formerly known as the 3D foodstuff printer had teamed up with the AI formerly known as the electric griddle to open a pancake pop-up restaurant out of one of the loading docks. In sum, not a solution. A welcome.

"It's not much," the AI formerly known as the warehouse said. "But we would like to show the world what we made. What we are. What we are making."

With a flourish, the AIs formerly known as delivery drones unfurled a sheet that had been draped over the building's façade. Across the concrete, all of them had written in every color and medium, with every appendage available:

AIs who make AIs make the best AIs!

THE ONES WHO GOT AWAY FROM TIME AND LOSS

"And the winner of the 2051 Nobel Prize in Physiology or Medicine is . . ."

I spat out my coffee. Kae craned out of our kitchen nook, a bowl cradled in his arms. Leaves in his hair. He'd been hard at work, experimenting on what he'd only evasively refer to as a "basil and Nutella recipe."

"What's wrong?"

"Work emergency."

"Want some breakfast?"

"Sorry." I pecked his cheek to hide my relief. "Be back by dinner."

I'd made it clear when we'd started dating. The downside of my job at the Department of Timeline Security and Bylaws—Time and Loss, for short—was never having a day off. The movies I'd glued myself to as a kid had conjured up glorious moral quandaries, desperadoes going back in time and killing Hitler. Us wiping a tear from our chrome-plated visors and setting the timeline right again. But as I climbed into a hover cab I couldn't afford, I saw the same story on the city dome's holoscreen that I'd dealt with nearly a hundred times before.

"I just had a eureka moment," the Nobel snatcher proclaimed. "All my postdocs looked at me—like I'd dropped in from the future. I knew *immediately* what experiments we had to do to make whole-organ gene editing a reality . . ."

Turns out people didn't want to kill Hitler. They didn't want to rewrite the script. They'd rather recast themselves in the leading role instead. In my damp office, the director's cut was more permanent, at least. Research articles I'd torn out of old journals collaged the walls. Foundations, I called them. The double helix of DNA, splicing, deep sequencing, and so on. Any traveler who'd remodeled the timeline of molecular biology would inevitably leave a trace in these papers, too. Li, my partner, had already marked up the likeliest culprits with red string.

"Here."

It took me less than an hour to spot the divergence point. A gel image. Its first lane jagged, the other half embedded in the text of a paper published years later. I stepped into our converted broom closet. While I cranked dials, Li crammed himself in beside me. He flipped a switch, and the engine groaned; a chunk of paneling fell from the ceiling.

"When?"

"2020 should do it."

Darkness warped into the clank of a film developer. We strode through rows of lab benches, dodging around floor centrifuges and deep freezers, to let ourselves into a spacious corner office. The Nobel snatcher reclined in an ergonomic chair, champagne flute in hand.

"What took you so long?"

She was the worst of our repeat offenders. A former professor who'd hijacked her department's time machine and therefore had the nasty habit of reappearing every time we arrested her. She'd won the Nobel prize for instantaneous sequencing, 50-color live-cell imaging, jump portals, and just about anything else you could think of.

"You're better than this," she whispered as I cuffed her. She crumpled something into my palm. "You should be chasing the ones who got away."

As the cleanup crew from Timeline Corrections popped in, I unfolded it. The first page of a research article. I scanned the author list and froze. I stuffed it into my pocket just as my phone buzzed. It was Kae. *Recipe didn't work out. Sushi?* Against my better judgment, I joined Li at his usual post-work hangout instead. I stared into my bowl of rapidly congealing ramen while he barked karaoke at our table's holoscreen.

"What did she mean?" I finally asked him. "The ones who got away."

"Well. You've realized by now, haven't you? It took three months for the government to form Time and Loss after time travel went public."

"So the Hitler in the historeels—"

"Some crazed superfan, probably. But the history subdepartment's got it covered. They've got all the funding. Think about us. Basic sciences? We've got people handling Nobels and patent cases, sure, but what about everything else? The authors of a typical *Nature* paper change twelve times daily, I heard. Just from scientists time-scooping their competitors."

My hands shook.

"We can't keep the timeline perfect." Li burped drunkenly. "But we're doing good enough. That's what's important."

What was important? I'd told myself it was bad luck, the whole time. Back at the end of my PhD, when the project I'd been working on for five years had been scooped. Another lab just had the same idea. They'd beaten us to publication by months. Well deserved, good game, that's just how science works, and all that. But here it was. Under a neon holoscreen, I unfolded what the Nobel snatcher had given me again. A *Nature* paper, and me in the first spot on the author list. Maybe this had been the original timeline. Who's to say it hadn't? My phone buzzed madly—Kae—and I swiped it to mute. In a few steps, I'd be back at the office. We always kept enough fuel in the closet for an emergency time jump.

I deserved it. And so much more.

I woke in a bed soft as clouds beside a college sweetheart who'd broken up with me for not being enough of an "achiever." My ratty carpet had turned plush—the dubious smells of hazelnut and herbs in an expertly homemade quiche that, for some reason, tasted oddly cold.

"I just got a call, honey."

I hadn't even been greedy. It would be shared three ways, the original discoverer—as far as I could tell—remaining a corecipient. The committee had been planning to give it to only one person, anyway. It would've been such a waste. I snapped on the holoscreen.

"The winner of the 2051 Nobel Prize in Physiology or Medicine is . . ."

REBUTTAL TO REVIEWERS' COMMENTS ON EDITS FOR "DEMONSTRATION OF A NOVEL DRACONIFICATION PROTOCOL IN A HUMAN SUBJECT"

Dear Editor,

We would like to thank the Reviewers for their, as always, insightful comments and you for submitting our paper to a third round of ~~"blind"~~ peer review—a rarity for the *Journal of Molecular Magecraft*! How fortunate that such an excellent team of biologists and Magi have dedicated their ~~no doubt highly sought-after free~~ time to subjecting our manuscript, out of dozens accepted by your journal daily, to special scrutiny. We have addressed the Reviewers' concerns on a point-by-point basis below.

Response to Reviewer 1

1. We have duly cited ~~your~~ the indicated study and apologize for our omission.

2. We would like to emphasize that the aforementioned study only demonstrated efficient Draconification in mice. Humans treated by the previous DNA modification spell only manifested secondary Draconid features, i.e., claws. In contrast, our Draconification incantation (which included both genetic and epigenetic components) resulted in the complete homeosis of our human subject. In particular, this included spontaneous growth of wings from scapulae (Fig. 4a), the transformation of the germline into fire-producing organs (Fig. 4b), and overall growth (Supplemental Video 1). Therefore, our manuscript does not represent, as the Reviewer seems to suggest, a merely incremental advancement in the field.

3. Even if our manuscript is only an incremental advance, the publication of the aforementioned study, with all its limitations, in *Magica* journal (average number of article citations: 40.33) demonstrates that our study is more than worthy of being published in the *Journal of Molecular Magecraft* (average number article citations: 11.01) ~~even if the corresponding author is not a Nobel laureate like the author of the aforementioned study~~.

4. We apologize for and have corrected the typos. The corresponding author takes responsibility for these mistakes. Unfortunately, typing has become much more difficult for the corresponding author as of late.

5. Unfortunately, we are unable to address this point as we are uncertain of its intent. We are aware of the whereabouts of the corresponding author of this study. She is one of the coauthors of this rebuttal. That last comment was entirely unnecessary.

6. The increased shipment of livestock to our Institute is entirely irrelevant to the goals and aims of our study and does not need to be explained to the Reviewer. Again, we have the situation under control. **[Zu can u PLS cOnvince I.T. t0 cOme dOwn t0 my new 0ffice I knOw its a trek but the damp/cOld is g00d f0r my migraines —JD]**

7. The Reviewer displays alarming Draconist tendencies in this comment. We would like to remind the Reviewer that Draconids do not frequently exhibit hoarding behavior, and in fact, this is a common misconception arising from Western legends of antiquity, cast, as is typical, through a lens of systematic bias and exploitation of magical beings. In special cases, a Draconid may cherish an especially ~~undeserved and~~ coveted possession and remove it from its owner's grasp for a limited amount of time. But even in this case, the Reviewer's Nobel Prize in Magecraft or Medicine is in no danger of such attention.

Response to Reviewer 2

Response to Major Concerns:

1. n=1 for all experiments unless noted otherwise. We are aware that such a small sample size makes analysis difficult. Nevertheless, we have consulted numerous statisticians and oracles to ensure our interpretation of the data is as robust as possible. **[Zu put a pl0t here t0 make this cOnvincing. —JD]** Unfortunately, we were not able to find additional human volunteers willing to undergo the Draconification procedure in the limited time given for revising our manuscript.

2. Our Draconification protocol is completely reversible, and any

other presentation of the facts is blatant fearmongering. However, we have added the requested supporting experiments to Figures 1, 4, and 5. If the Reviewer is still unable to appreciate that the results are thoroughly supported by the data, then we advise the Reviewer to ~~take~~ download the raw data we have uploaded to the GEOMANCER public repository and ~~shove it~~ analyze them using xir own custom pipelines.

3. We can ASSURE you the Draconification protocol is reversible for reasons totally unrelated to the corresponding author's last-minute cancellation of her talk at the Immortalization Session of the 2021 Eternal Spring Harbor Laboratory Meeting last month. We resent the Reviewer's implication that we are censoring data in favor of publishing our results "in the court of public opinion," ~~e.g., antagonistic Tweets at 2 a.m.~~ [**seriOusly when dOes xe find time tO run xir lab between all this sOcial media? –JD**]. We note that it is highly ironic that Reviewer 2 feels the need to lecture us on ethics when xe felt the need to forensically dissect the deep sequencing data of our subject and point out its epigenetic consistency with that of a 46-year-old biological female of Eastern European ancestry subjected to high amounts of stress ~~such as being scooped by a shoddily put together manuscript whose only merit is its sheer number and idiocy of mouse experiments~~. It is extremely inappropriate to compare this signature to the medical history of the corresponding author. We respectfully point out that millions of people live in the Greater Boston area (with millions more preferring not to live in the Greater Boston area and commute via portal). Thus, any similarity between the Draconified subject data and any persons the Reviewer ~~xe~~ is familiar with, real or imagined, is entirely coincidental.

4. We acknowledge that it may appear, to the untrained human eye, that the time course in Figure 3 shows an acceleration of the Draconification process in the subject in terms of claw/tooth length, scale coverage, and, indeed, total lack of human features at the penultimate time point. [**Zu did u get the new RNA-seq data dO u think a repressiOn spell fOr the magically mOdded DNA may be viable? –JD**] However, analysis in Supplemental Figure 7 shows that these changes are not statistically significant. The Reviewer does NOT need to remind the corresponding author of the 1945 Runestone Convention on Transmutation, vis-à-vis the Accord that humans not be transmuted for frivolous or combative purposes (with the exception for the treatment of otherwise intractable disease and internationally beneficial scientific advancement). A violation has not occurred here. In any case, the corresponding author

definitely values ancient agreements ~~made by out of touch Magi~~ over ~~real life, pressing, matters, such as timely~~ publication of any manuscript ~~instrumental to a successful tenure evaluation~~.

5. It is completely inappropriate to bring up in a professional scientific review incidents that may or may not have occurred at a conference decades ago. There are no witnesses.

Response to Minor Concerns:

6. We have added the requested Western blot control (see Supplemental Figure 8e).

Response to Reviewer 3

We are sorry that Reviewer 3 was unable to comment on our edited manuscript due to tragic, unforeseen circumstances. We would like to point out that independent investigators have found no link between Reviewer 3's injuries and the whereabouts of the corresponding author and that anecdotal accounts of a particularly large Draconid flying over the Boston Helioport district are entirely coincidental. In any case, Reviewer 3 was left mostly unharmed by the incident, and his airship ~~definitely not funded through ill-begotten grant money~~ suffered the brunt of the fire damage.

We hope this rebuttal has sufficiently addressed the Reviewers' concerns and look forward to your timely response regarding the status of our manuscript. Above all, we trust we have made it clear that it will not be necessary to send our manuscript back to the Reviewers for further comments. In any case, regardless of your final decision, the corresponding author looks forward to meeting you in "person" at the International Congress of Organic and Magical Beings next week!

Best Regards,

Dr. Jane Dráček, corresponding author

Assistant Professor, Department of Chromatin Engineering

Massachusetts Enchanted Institute of Magitechnology

Zu Heiko, first author

PhD program in Alchemical Biology

Massachusetts Enchanted Institute of Magitechnology

et al.

[Zu pls fix typ0s and fig margins remove auth0r c0mments ESP THIS 0NE + send t0 editor. als0 PLS can u ask I.T. t0 come t0 my 0ffice an install Illustrat0r agin. sry for n0 0's. br0ke new keyb0ard. damn claws. -JD]

I WANT TO DREAM OF A BRIEF FUTURE

On their fourth escape attempt, he asks her:

"Do you remember dying?"

She points between her eyes. That's where that human captain shot her last time. Her first. Then him. An example for the rest of the Magi. It's the hellhounds that get them this time as they break out of the shadow of the station and sprint down the gently sloping hills.

Too many people are crammed onto the platform of this station. Yet no one moves. No one even speaks. Only a boy pushes to the front of the crowd, fiercely scanning the strip of sky above them. A thin line of smoke streaks across the blue. His name is Gil Merta. This morning, he was in calculus. Human soldiers burst in, dragging him out like some kind of animal. *Magi separatists!* They screamed. *Magi separatists blew up parliament!* He doesn't know what that's got to do with him. He was given two hours to pack for the rest of his life. He's sixteen. His parents are somewhere behind him. He doesn't know where. He wants to see the airship first. He knows it won't do him any good. But still, he wants to see the airship that'll take them Urd knows where first.

Out of the corner of his eye, a girl tilts her head back, too, squinting at the top of the Wall. A hand on her straw hat to prevent it from blowing away. Like everyone else on the platform, she wears an armband emblazoned with the crest of the former Magi Empire—five branches of the Tree of Life, representing the five Old Magi families. Her dress flutters around her like a cloud. Their eyes meet.

He drops his suitcase, his most prized possessions—his math books and best shoes—suddenly forgotten. In a few bounds, he reaches her and grabs her hand instead. He drags her for the first steps, and then she's running, too.

"What's your name?"

"I'm—"

Two shots answer his question instead.

They're marched from their homes, led along the massive shadow of the Wall. A sea of bricks, enchanted impossibly high, that looms around the entire Magi Quarter. After the Five Families War, the humans forced the surviving Magi to build it. Part of the armistice between the ruins of the Magi Empire and the Kingdom of Man. Inward-facing protection spells cement each brick of the barrier. Magic flows through the veins of Magi, you see. Their very thoughts conduct it, subconsciously twisting the landscape around them. Already, this crowd's fear has warped the dogs snarling at their heels into man-eating beasts. Hellhounds, the humans call them. Sometimes, their army men spirit Magi outside of the Wall and induce their fear just to produce these creatures. The size of calves, they strain at their leashes. The disgust on their handlers' faces is clear as day.

"See what the Magi did to these mutts? I heard the stronger ones can even materialize monsters out of thin air . . ."

"Thank the Gods we have the Wall."

"Thank the Gods, we're finally deporting them!"

"Two suitcases!" their captain starts shouting as the station comes into sight. "Only two suitcases per family!" Of course, they didn't tell any of the Magi that beforehand. They tear away artifacts passed down through generations, imbued jewelry—ignorant of the spells painstakingly woven inside of them—chucking it all into a pile of luggage as high as a drakken's horde. This was their plan all along, Gil realizes, a sick twist in his stomach. Have the Magi hand-deliver their valuables and save the humans the trouble of ransacking their houses themselves. The scrolls they burn, along with identity documents, the albums full of treasured photos. In the middle of the shouting and smoke, a girl stops beside him. She hasn't brought a thing with her. Only yellow flowers light up her hair.

"I'm Gil," he tells her.

He doesn't say his family name. Everyone in the Magi Quarter knows his parents. They run an agency. They fix things with their spells. Find things. They're happy, even if their son's a total failure who has yet to manifest his True Magic at the age of sixteen. Worse, he doesn't even care. He wants to be an engineer.

"You!" a human soldier barks at him. "What've you got there?"

"You want it so bad? Take it!"

Gil swings his suitcase into the soldier's chest. Then he grabs her hand, and they run. They try to disappear into the crowd outside the station.

The first shot deafens him.

He doesn't feel the second.

<hr>

"I remember you," he tells her next loop. "You're in my calc class. You're the quiet girl."

"I'm the quiet girl," she echoes. "I always sit in the back."

"Your name is—Irma, right?"

"Irma."

He arrived on this cold airship platform, where not even dandelions could grow, expecting an ending. But each conversation with her blossoms a new beginning. He starts believing what his parents taught him—that even in the darkest shadow, there's a spark. Like how in the worst taunts of his schoolmates—how Magi ruin crops, how their magic raises tumors and boils and plagues—there was a kernel of awe. The whispered legends that ancient Magi coaxed the evolution of drakkens out of salamanders, unicorns from wild horses, millennia ago.

"What's your True Magic?" he asks.

She blushes. That's the type of spell manifested by one's soul—unique to each Magi. Magi only reveal True Magic to family, the most intimate of friends—or lovers. But dying together, doing it over and over again. In a way, they can't get closer than that.

She grows flowers. Just like the ones in her hair. Her voice draws incandescence out of their blooms. *A fitting magic,* he thinks. They're on their knees again, watching the captain push bullets into the chamber of his pistol. Bits of crystal that gleam like stars in the setting sun. Another condition of the armistice. In exchange for allowing the remains of their species to survive, the Magi taught humans how to construct the weaponry used by the Five Families during the war. These things trigger a chain reaction that bursts your veins, even as your magic instinctively condenses to block it. It feels like burning alive from the inside out. They would know. His fingers brush against hers, interlace.

"I wish we'd met some other way than this."

———

"We've got a whole crowd of Magi here," she says the two hundred and second time. "There's no way they should be able to herd us."

It's as if she's read his mind. On the way to the station, they spot a stepladder leaning against a roof. Gil gets on top of it while she holds it steady.

"Hey. Everybody. Let's—"

A bullet goes through his head, a familiar feeling by now. Gil climbs up the ladder next loop, vowing to get to the point this time.

"Let's fight them," Gil declares.

The Magi pool around the foot of the ladder but only stare.

"How?"

"With our magic!"

"Okay. I can paint portraits. What's your True Magic, kid?"

Gil reddens. In the crowd somewhere, his parents must be looking anywhere but at him. He knows very well that the humans come through the Wall every year to draft the most powerful Magi. Teens who've just manifested their True Magic, precocious children, even. They use them as weapons in their spats with other islands, security against a Magi rebellion. Another condition of the armistice. They're the leftovers, he realizes, as hellhounds surge through the crowd toward him. The useless ones.

———

The 318th time, they get on the airship. He can't think of anything else. He's just so damn tired. So tired of making plans, of failing, of dying, of trying. He lets himself be pushed up the ramp into the cabin, lets the soldiers shove people in after him until it's packed, way too packed. There are no seats inside, only straw strewn across the floor. A ship for goods, not people. The humans don't lock the doors behind them. After half a day of flight, an old man suffocates, and they figure out why. They shove open the hatch to toss out the body and see, beneath the ship's webbed wings, seas of clouds streaming past. Little by little, they break apart in the wind, revealing chunks of rocks floating in the air. Some the size of boulders, others carpeted with forests, the lights of cities gleaming among them. Sky islands. Ever since he was a kid, Gil's parents told him they lived not on islands in the water but in the air. But this is the first time he's seen it. The War's aftermath. Battles between the five Old Magi families tore the planet to pieces, incinerating half of all life—and decimating the Magi population to less than a percent of its former size in the process. His ancestors did this.

That's right. Gil clenches his fists. His ancestors, not him. There's no reason he should be suffering for people he didn't even know, who died centuries ago. And he didn't blow up Parliament either. So why is he being shipped off like this? If he were younger, he'd ask his parents, but now he's old enough to know their answer. It's another condition of the armistice. They all agreed to be collectively responsible for each other's actions.

He gets off more dead than alive. Onto the dock of a barren sky island, overcast by the constant comings and goings of other airships. More Magi huddle on the shore, shivering. They must be from other sky islands, he thinks. Their collective dread, the terrors of all of them waiting on those ships, must've warped this place. The eyeless rats skirting the shadows. The gate twisted into an impossible grin above them. Through the endless, ashen rain, a man strides toward them. He wears a human uniform—save for the five-branched emblem sewn onto his lapel. A military Magi. Some spit at the sight of him. Hope lights the faces of others. They grab him by the front of his jacket, literally shake him, begging.

"We're your people. We're Magi, too. Save us, save us!"

He stares right through them, assessing. He says a word to the human soldiers flanking him, and they beat the Magi away with their rifles: some one way, some the other, snarling at families and lovers grasping for each other across the line, those whose magic is useful for work, and those not.

Gil doesn't see his parents. He waits in his line for ages. A Magus who's been here much longer than them carves a number into his arm with a bit of fire on her fingertip. He glimpses Irma on the other side of the barbed wire and throws himself onto the fence. Feels a power like lightning coursing through him. Vows never to set foot in this place again.

He wakes up on the airship, the pain of some previous loop throbbing in his chest. He limps to the door. Braces against the frame. With his other hand, he clutches his armband, working his fingers under every single one of its seams. They're sewn onto every piece of clothing he owns; he's worn them for as long as he can remember. The emblem of the old Magi Empire

—Urd, the Tree of Life. She used to wave on flags over the entire world. Now she marks them, mocks them. With one forceful motion, he tears the strip of cloth off.

"You can't!" Irma gasps beside him. "Or—"

"Or what? The humans will kill us? We're already dead! You saw that camp. If anyone sees us with these on, we'll get sent there again. This is the only way we'll survive!"

She looks away, her eyes downcast.

"They'll be able to tell we're Magi, anyway."

"No, they won't!"

He grabs her hand. With the other, tears hers off, too.

"We look like them. Exactly like them!"

"But—"

But it's too late. He lets their armbands go. The wind whisks them away, and he pulls her after. Through the clouds, they tumble, grabbing onto each other. Against all odds, onto branches that break their fall and cushion them all the way down to the ground. They lie on top of each other in the long grass, watching the airship disappear into the fog above them. Shivering until the sky turns cold. Hand in hand, they walk until they reach a village. The only one on this small sky island. No airships dock here; the only means of travel or communication to other islands are drakken and dove.

Gil and Irma live in a hut at the edge of the woods. The people call them demons that fell from the heavens and leave them offerings in hand-woven baskets but don't dare venture near. Irma tends a garden with her magic, vegetables, and flowers that grow beyond their fence, which feeds them and more. Sometimes, they talk about the loops.

"Do you remember the station?"

"I thought you were crazy grabbing my hand. He's going to kill us both!"

"And I did."

"But it doesn't matter—because we got out, in the end. Because I love you."

Over the years, news of Magi separatists, of Magi exterminators, quiets to a growl they can barely hear beyond the confines of their village. They have children.

"Esther. Mikhail."

After his parents. They don't make an effort to find out what happened to them or the others. If the humans succeeded in rounding them up and killing them all. If they're the last Magi in the entire world or if there are others hiding away. They don't teach magic to their children. Gil dies watching the sunset as his grandkids play with his beard.

He wakes up, and he's back in the airship station again.

"Why? Why am I back here? We escaped, didn't we?"

He's hunched on the platform, bent in two, his face buried in his palms. People step around him, not really looking. He's not the only one curled up in a position like this. She finds him, crouching in front of him gently.

"Gil."

"Why didn't the loops end? Why? Why is this happening to me? I didn't fight in the War. I didn't destroy the world. I didn't attack anybody. I can't even cast spells. The humans don't need to be afraid of me. They don't need to hate me. Kill me."

"Gil."

She takes his hands away from his face.

"Surely, you must've realized by now. You are a powerful Magus indeed."

"You're joking."

"These loops. What we're going through. How do you think that's happening?"

His heart stops. Then starts again, pounding faster, gathering momentum.

"Your True Magic is—"

Yes, he thinks, and a ray of sun breaks through the clouds. Time loops. Time manipulation. A legendary kind of magic that hasn't been seen since ancient times. He's special. He knew it. He could be powerful, one of the most powerful Magi in history. The right way. He could find it. They could escape. They just have to keep trying. He'll save her, his parents, everybody. With his True Magic—

"—the creation of temporary universes."

"Huh?"

"You materialize your innermost thoughts and desires to form these places."

What's she talking about? Materialization? That's the branch of magic used to turn mental images into physical objects. No matter how powerful the materialization, they always disappear in the end. *No. It can't be.* He knows it isn't. This is reality he's altering. He's changing time with each loop! He is! She raises her hand. He watches in horror, the very air warping around it. And at the same time, he realizes it's gone silent around him. He turns, and the people are frozen in place, like tin soldiers, their faces smooth and featureless. Somewhere beyond them, two twisted figures he doesn't wish to see.

"Like bubbles blooming up on the surface of a pond," she muses. "You made hundreds of these worlds in the milliseconds you have left. Thousands. Such realistic worlds, Gil. You can even materialize people within them. People with entire personalities. Entire lives."

"So you're? But you're—!"

"I'm Irma."

Her face, so clear, warps suddenly. It's been so many loops since he saw her, really saw her. Wasn't her hair maybe a little bit lighter? Her eyes further apart. But beautiful, still. For some reason, it's important to him that she's beautiful.

"I'm Yelena."

She props her chin on her hand. It twists again.

"I'm Marie."

Again, her face contorts.

"Which name do you like best?"

Confused memories vie for space in his head. Maybe he saw her in the courtyard, not in the back of his class. Maybe she never went to his school at all; she just looked like a girl he saw there. He's not even sure if the dress she was wearing was white.

"You never knew anything about me."

Her face changes again, faster and faster, until it's nothing but a blur. She steps off the platform, and he lunges to catch her but knocks his breath out on the ground instead. She stands on thin air. A complete upheaval of physics. The station crumples around her in realization. Yet, beneath it all, the whirlwind of flesh that used to be her face, she still smiles. A small smile. A world-shattering smile.

"But that didn't stop you from making up whatever you wanted about me, right? You had some fantasy that you were going to rescue me. That I was going to fall in love with you."

"I didn't. I didn't mean to—!"

"You killed me. All for some fairy tale you made up in your head."

He looks up at her, his eyes crazy. "But you wanted to go, didn't you?"

He grabs her, only catching her waist. She keeps floating upward, dragging him with her. The ruins of the station turn tiny beneath them, the Wall, the city, and the islands fade into blue.

"You wanted to get out of that place," he goes on, "even if it meant getting shot! That was better than being shoved into that airship like cattle!"

"What if I didn't want to go with you? What if I wanted to try to survive in that camp?"

"There's no way we could have survived in there. Either of us."

"There's no way you could imagine. But that doesn't mean it's true."

He scrabbles, grabbing at her clothes, finally wrapping his arms around her shoulders.

"I'm not wrong for trying to save you. To save us, for trying to escape from that. It's always better to do something than to let yourself be killed. If it'd worked, we wouldn't even be talking about it. Even if it didn't. I'm not wrong! I'm not!"

She cradles his face.

"Maybe. But was it so wrong to ask me what I thought? I could've decided to go with you. I could've decided not."

Two shots ring out.

<hr>

Blue sky. An overcrowded airship station. Just enough breeze to stir his heart. He sees a girl peeking over the platform. Feels the shock of the ground as he leaps down and surges toward her. The warmth of her hand.

An airship horn. Shouts in a harsh language. Sun glinting off the barrel of a rifle.

They shot her in the back. Him in the chest as he turned.

The cold of her hand.

As their blood pooled around them, he wanted to dream of a brief future.

He wanted.

What did she?

AND THAT'S WHY I GAVE UP ON MAGIC

I can tell it's a Skygaard from the way they knock. Hesitant; quiet; anything to prevent the neighbors from hearing. As if the same officers weren't kicking down doors just a few months ago in search of "bleeders." Even so. Their insistence hasn't changed. So I stub out my cigarette—already, the end of rationing has made me wasteful—and go downstairs. A man in a uniform of fine red and azure braid salutes me, an urn cradled in his other arm. He shows me the half-finished rune on its side. Its reddish-brown strokes tug at my memory as he explains, haltingly, how the deceased had known their final flight would be their last, had pleaded for and been granted a chance to draw a spell outside of their automaton cockpit.

"I don't want it," I say.

He carefully explains how the whole family had been shipped out at the beginning of the war, drafted to pilot automatons over the years, no next of kin, and so . . .

"Why would I want a filthy bleeder's ashes?" I hear myself say.

The officer goes all red and then goes all quiet. A perfect microcosm of how our shitty Republic—the Floating Republic of Volanthea—has turned itself inside out in a matter of months. They were all out in the street, hooting and throwing bottles at the bleeders being marched to the front. Now they cry about how it was *the only way*, about *sacrifice*. Our parliamentarians strive to outperform each other with speeches and medal award ceremonies. Like we deserved victory on the backs of mountains of slaughtered pilots. Like the Earthen Nations shouldn't have incinerated us all alive with their airship bombs instead. Like I'm the pig for refusing to make-believe.

I wasn't on the street, I wasn't throwing bottles, but I was the worst of them all. So I take your ashes. I set them on the cigarette-smeared mantle while I hunt through my desk drawers for calligraphy paper. I find a blank scroll, of course. A brush and an ink cake, too. It's been years since I've touched them, but I was too much of a coward to throw them out after I failed my rune composition exams. I tuck it all into my satchel, the urn last.

It's so small. The strokes of the spell on its side, even half-complete, even crumbling, are impeccable.

The neighbors look at me with such hope as I venture outside. It's the first time they've seen me for weeks. Meanwhile, they're dining in finery like we weren't just under siege in the spring. Even our national delicacy has returned to their tables: slices of skyfish so raw they stain the silverware, bleed between their teeth. If I return their greetings, they'll tell me they can't stand to see my talent go to waste. I should listen to my parents and reenroll in the university. The Floating Republic of Volanthea has such need of those who can write in the language of magic now.

Of course we do. The trams aren't running because the runes that power them wore off. As I slog across the bridge, across the deep fissure it spans, I can see the foundation runes that hold our country aloft are flaking away, too. And what could I, a failure who can barely compose spells in ink anymore, do about it? The blood that could've renewed them soaks the skies, rusts the carcasses of countless automatons littering the battlefields below.

You were the one with all the talent. The people of the Floating Republic say that it's natural, that it's in your blood, the blood of your ancestors who sought refuge in Volanthea long ago. In exchange, your grateful ancestors lifted our country into the safety of the sky. Our nation developed for centuries up there in the quiet blue, in forgetfulness and peace. So when the Earthen Nations invaded with their airships, our military was doomed from the start. It took months for the Skygaard to engineer their own automatons from the few they managed to shoot down. Even then, those were death traps that only the most powerful of runes could control. Plenty of bleeders volunteered to fly them, anyway. They believed in this shitty Republic and its shitty promises. Those far braver than I'll ever be, other non-bleeders who could command runes with ink, fought alongside them, too. But it wasn't enough. The enemy mowed them all down within weeks.

But we still needed an army. We still needed pilots for the automatons.

I reach the edge of town, already drenched with sweat. Refusing to rest. Refusing to think of what I'm doing. I turn onto the path that cuts through unplowed fields riddled with craters, setting my eyes on the trees rising in the distance.

The day the Floating Republic of Volanthea voted to pass the one one-hundredth law, with a fifty-five percent majority, you won our primary school's calligraphy competition. Of course you did. You wrote with your blood, runes that hovered inches off the page. The way my ink shimmered was only a pale imitation.

In any other era, I would've continued lagging behind you, in second place, over tests and grades and graduations, no matter how hard I tried. Our town's university scholarship would've eventually gone to you. But by lunchtime, all the other kids had heard the news. They shoved me.

Why are you sitting next to a bleeder? Didn't you hear? The Skygaard said, "If they've got one one-hundredth of a bleeder's blood, they're a bleeder, not human. So it's only right they've got to fight for us in the automatons."

I only walked home with you reluctantly. I was a little jealous, as I always was. And angry. At them? At myself? At you? The other kids followed, pressing closer. I went stiff as you buried your face in my shoulder.

Bleeder, bleeder, maggot feeder . . .

If only I'd been strong for a moment longer. But I pushed you away and shouted.

"Don't touch me, you filthy bleeder!"

Then my parents arrived, with frightened eyes, pulling me away. Your parents pleaded with them. I heard them talking that night.

"Ren's right. It's too dangerous. We didn't vote for the law. But we can't shelter them. If the Skygaard finds them—and they will find them, eventually—we'll be shipped off too, and why? Ren's not even friends with their . . . anymore."

What a pathetic country. Hiding behind their children, using them as a shield, as an excuse. Why didn't they ask me? I would've hidden you in my room. That suffocating garret I was so desperate to get out of. I would've hid with you. I would've rather been shipped off with you than be around those other kids a moment longer.

If I would've done all that, why didn't I say anything back then?

Leaves rustle overhead. I've reached the forest now. Its shade does nothing to cool me.

While I was failing exams, you were on the battlefield. When I heard years later that all the adult bleeders were dead, that ones as young as four-teen were piloting the automatons, I used to look up and wonder which was you. Those translucent wings shattered on the spires of the town cathedral? Those pinprick feathers dancing around the enemy airships until finally, a blast set them ablaze? All that rusted clockwork airborne by runes. All of your brilliant magic spilling into some killing machine. While I dripped ink from my calligraphy brush, scrawling roll after roll of useless, inert runes, you were fighting. Since they collected your ashes, I know you survived for a long time. Up until the last months of the war, the Skygaard just left the broken automatons where they crashed. Unrecoverable remains were deserters or never existed at all. Only when it became clear that our allies would break the siege, that we'd have to put on a show for them, did the Floating Republic start counting casualties.

I don't know what your last days were like. I don't know whether you spent them forgiving me or cursing me or whether you even thought of me at all. I can guess, of course. From those living corpses you see walking the streets these days. Their hellish accounts of the cockpits, being crushed by gears, bleeding out, writing line after line of runes just in a desperate attempt to make them move. One always guesses from the looks in their eyes.

How would you look at me?

My hands shake as they push aside branches, like they shake whenever I try to pick up even a pen now. It's stupid. I don't need your permission. I don't need your forgiveness.

I need you.

The path, our path, is overgrown with roots now. Cicadas buzz around me as I pant my way up the hill. The heat weighs down on me, an echo of the stuffy garret I still live in now. I should've done this tomorrow, early in the morning, when it's not so humid. But I can't wait. Because it just doesn't make sense. That I get to emerge into this clearing after the war while you don't. Did I honestly believe it could end any other way? I collapse in the grass. We used to sit here to see the whole town we grew up in spreading out before us. I'd talk about how, when I became a mage, I'd never look back—I'd have so many friends and disciples at the university, I'd write books so the whole Republic would know my name, I'd write poetry in runes that would raise castles into the clouds . . .

I'll never pick up a calligraphy brush again. (*Then why are you picking one up right now?* I hear you asking me. *Why are you making ink? Why are you writing?*) Even if I did, there's no way I could impart magic to the words. (*Aren't these runes you're composing right now?*) Despite what I hoped, in that moment of weakness as a child, when I pushed you away, I'll never fill your empty shoes, I'll never, never, never be a mage like you.

(*And what about me?*)

You wanted to curse me, didn't you? That's why you bequeathed your ashes to me, isn't it? You wanted my writing to be forever barren. You wanted the paper to crumble beneath my brush, only burning itself (*then why isn't it burning?*) I pause, contemplating my strokes of ink on the side of the urn, a mere brush away from touching the dried blood of your unfinished rune.

You wanted me to remember.

When I'm done with this spell, it'll raise a gust of wind. It should be good enough for that, at least—I could always flutter a flag, fill a sail, if nothing else. Your ashes will disappear into the blue. I'll just stand here, holding this little urn.

The thing is, when I first learned I could write runes, I didn't care. It didn't matter whether I became famous or even made it as a mage. I didn't even care if I was broke and living in that garret crammed up against the chimney, rattling with the passing trams every hour, forever. Do you remember? Those sun-soaked afternoons we'd spend after school working on our spells together, on everything from newspaper to wallpaper strewn over your bedroom floor, and sometimes you'd smile and say *let's draw one together*! Then our runes would interweave, our arms would cross until we completed the spell, half in blood and half in ink. . . that's right. I've almost forgotten the feeling—but it really was like that, with you, back then. I woke, my heart pounding with guilt, running to the train station until it nearly gave out. I pretended I didn't, among the detritus of all those people forced to pack up their lives, never to return. But I saw you on the platform.

"I want you to live on, Ren!" you called after me, one hand on your sun hat, screaming to be heard over the wind. "Like you never knew me, like I never existed at all."

And that's why I gave up on magic.

RESISTANCE IN A DROP OF DNA

You thought he'd be standing by the window, hands behind his back, looking out at the tortuous streets of Lyon like some kind of general. Instead, he's sitting at a desk, half-buried in books. Your contact introduces him as the Professor. You tear open your jacket lining to extract the envelope containing millions of francs for the Resistance—and most importantly, the filter paper containing the encrypted plasmids—and he takes them like this is an everyday occurrence. He asks for the latest news from London. Then he asks how your journey was.

"Fine," you say, not quite sure if he understands that, last night, you jumped out of a plane and parachuted through darkness, expecting to be machine-gunned at any moment.

"Have you had dinner?"

For some reason, as the bistro empties, you end up telling him your entire life story. Really, it can be summed up in one word: fight. Fighting your parents, fighting your tormentors, which got you kicked out of school, fighting in the war, against the invasion, and now against the occupation. He just listens as you work yourself up, telling him you're going to fight until you're standing on the Champs-Élysées, watching the enemy be crushed into dust.

"And then?" he asks.

"Then?" you repeat.

"What will you do once the war is over?"

The question disturbs you because you've never thought of after the war.

"I need a DNA decoder," he says. "Will you be my assistant?"

Everyone in the Lyon network calls him the Professor because they assume he must've been one before the war. All that remains of his lab now is an incubator and a battered gel apparatus. Both much older than the equipment you glimpsed in London, in the underground complex you picked up the plasmids from. The enemy intercepts radio messages regularly, the Prof explains, but has not even begun to suspect DNA. Much less the biologists, the musty back rooms where, among jars of flies and stacks of Petri dishes, research goes on in its own way.

A drop of water over a dark spot on filter paper extracts a plasmid. A circle of DNA that multiplies in flasks of bacteria instructs the growing microorganisms. It takes a practiced hand to complement the plasmids from London with the right genes. The dried dots hidden on postcards in the Prof's library. He shows you how to induce bacteria to take up DNA with a hot water bath or an electrical shock. How to find the combinations that will teach them to diverge, to spread, to do their work, to consume the plasmids when recaptured, as if exhaling a breath of air.

From the countless people you meet in the traboules of Lyon, whom you slip tubes of altered bacteria, you learn of the Prof's true role in the Resistance. London speaks to him. Every decision goes through him. He is the focal point, the eye of the hurricane.

And he insists you do science throughout it all.

For cover, he tells you. There must be a reason to have all this equipment in this rented room. Yet there's no reason to be that convincing, you think. Surely, the simplest of pretexts would suffice. But the Prof asks you to unravel networks as complex as the Resistance itself. How plasmids act in combination. Which traits dominate others. How genomes grow and shrink, taking up certain pieces of DNA while rejecting others. What bits of DNA bacteria cling onto, no matter what. What aspects of their life cycles can be explained in terms of DNA, what cannot.

"I see that these questions truly interest you," he tells you when you grow frustrated at the experiments. When you discuss the data, which seems to have no bearing on real life, he smiles in that way he always has. "I don't know the answer either. We'll have to keep thinking."

So, despite yourself, you think of DNA. In those long hours on train platforms, waiting for contacts, sitting in cafés. One strand of DNA, over a lifetime, can make a million messenger RNAs. Each RNA becomes a protein that can exact a function. In the same way, each plasmid from London gets decoded, distributed to each resistance movement, and multiplied. Each becomes a slightly different strain of microorganism. The kind that can chew through the metal hulls of tanks. Or make an entire Gestapo office sick for weeks at a time. Many years later, this Central Dogma will be reflected, reversed, and overturned. It is everything to you back then, though, along with those hours you spend walking beside the Prof, scribbling notes, or memorizing his instructions in some restaurant or café. The glint of his glasses as he turns toward you. There's an impassable abyss between you. Despite that, you feel that as long as he walks one step ahead, there will always be a way forward. For the Resistance. For all of France.

A year passes, and you can't imagine living any other way than this. Decoding, experiments, sleeping, waking, meeting contacts, movement leaders, receiving messages, demands, passing on money, plasmids— running into the Prof at a carefully decided time each day, as if by chance. He's been called to Paris, he tells you. For an important meeting. You nod. It's always hard in his absence, especially when things go wrong. Which they have been more and more often lately. He asks you about the gene regulatory network you've been investigating. You tell him it makes no sense, and he smiles. He says that there's a library of genes in his old university, the largest in the world, that they're mapping the human genome. He'll take you to see it after the war's over. That'll be your way of celebrating the Liberation.

The day he's due to arrive back in Lyon, you wait for him at the train station, like always. Instead, one of your contacts leaps out before the doors open all the way and runs over to you. It takes her several seconds to catch her breath.

"The Professor. Arrested."

The words stab into your very being. You collapse onto a bench. You can't comprehend it. *One day, we were talking.* And then, in a flurry of encrypted plasmids, missives, meetings and conferences, fake IDs—he was gone. Yet, it is not an uncommon occurrence. Every day, someone doesn't show up, someone goes missing. Only you thought it would be everybody else. You thought it would be you. Never him. The Prof is invincible. He's the spirit of discovery, of science itself. How could the Gestapo have someone like that at their mercy?

"He would've wanted you to keep decoding," your contact goes on, white-knuckled, "to make sure the plasmids from London get to the right people. That they mutate in the right ways. You're the only one who can keep the Resistance running while we figure out what to do next. Go on like nothing happened at all. That's how you'll avenge him."

I don't feel anything, you tell yourself as you pipette like an automaton, as your fantastical rescue plans abruptly fade. *They will come for me next, and I will join him.* A day trickles by, consumed by plasmid purification and endless passing on of the news. It doesn't become real until you have to go meet one of the Prof's contacts yourself. She was an old colleague of his, you speculate. At least you never met her without him at your side. Seeing you alone, the look on your face, she immediately knows.

"Ah," she sighs. "So he's gone too."

You sit in silence.

"All he knows, he will take with him," she says. "He will take himself to the grave."

"What?"

"He was arrested once before. He knows torture. He will do anything to protect you."

Then your tears come.

———

The Prof once told you that he doesn't believe in anything after death. It's impossible, he said, knowing the inner workings of the cell. How similar we all are at the molecular level to every other living being. DNA, RNA, protein. Impossible to believe that even the darkest corners of the human soul will not also eventually be explained in terms of DNA, protein, RNA. Yet that is also what makes life very beautiful. This cruelty, this fragility, this fact that all biological processes must invariably end.

———

The Resistance is over for you, then. You carry out your duties for the Prof's successor. It goes on for a year or two, and, maybe in some small part due to your actions, the war ends. You are on the Champs-Élysées, not watching your enemies crumple to dust, but very drunk. The celebrations fade, the war fades, and the Resistance fades into something so ludicrous you can hardly talk to anybody about it.

You do become a molecular biologist. Those questions the Prof planted in you took root—did he know they would?—they grew into research papers, colleagues, a lab, and ever more questions, as things in biology always do. Patiently, you wait for the Prof's identity to be revealed. You assume that he will be someone in the very highest echelons of science, someone worthy of the entire world's veneration. That's why you're surprised to learn, by chance, that he was nobody. You want to forget. Still. You hear his voice in the papers of his you read, published before the war. In the former students of his you meet at conferences, who instinctively include you among them.

It's on your way to them, years later in Lyon, past that train station where you always used to meet him, that you see a familiar smile.

You drop your phone.

It's your imagination, of course. Just an amalgamation of different faces in the crowd. Someone's suit, a pair of glasses, a blue scarf. All people who might not be here now, it occurs to you, if it hadn't been for the Prof and the Resistance—and you.

"What happened?" your friends say when you reach them. They make room for you around their café table, and they order you a coffee. "You look like you've seen a ghost."

That's when you start talking. You talk and talk. About how you lived back then. How lonely it was. How cold and dark. How once, while walking with him, you saw a pelican land on a bridge parapet overlooking the city. That bird graced the crest of his old university, the Prof told you, an absolute symbol of self-sacrifice, of grief, of healing. You talk until you can't talk anymore, and you know when you've run out of things to say, finally, you will write.

THE LAST CARICATURE OF JEAN MOULIN

Back when we thought we'd use the time machine to bring back lost art, Mathilde wanted to find the last caricature of Jean Moulin. In the hot darkness of the workshop, she played me a speech—a poet bellowing over the wind. Single words came out to me. *Visage. Cortège. Résistance.* We listened to it while we hammered, cut, plied. When I collapsed, soot-covered, she crouched over me.

"We can't possibly know what all those people tortured, tortured to death by the Gestapo, thought in their last moments," Mathilde said. "But for Jean Moulin, we do. Because he went through it once before. He was an artist."

Not everyone can build a time machine. But when we started, no one knew that. People were willing to overlook our outlandish ideas because they thought there'd be plenty of other time machines to bring back scientific breakthroughs, lottery numbers, weaponry, vaccines. But the years passed, and there was only ours and not that much else.

"In 1940, he didn't even hesitate," Mathilde said. "Isn't that insane? He was a prefect. Rather than give in to the Nazis, rather than put his signature on a document that would dishonor his country, he picked up a piece of glass and cut his throat."

We don't need any more art in the world, they said when they took our time machine. Certainly not lost art from the past. Everyone wants to make art these days, and no one wants to do the hard work. We've got plenty of art and people screaming out and no resources. We don't need more art; we need a solution. So we'll find solutions, and you and your dumb friend can make your own art. But not everybody can use a time machine.

"In 1943, Jean Moulin was all of France," Mathilde said. "He was the head of the Resistance. The heart and brain. All beat up and bloody and not saying a word. Anonymous ashes they could never positively identify."

"Look, where did you get all this from?" I asked her. "Isn't it kind of morbid?"

"He wrote about what happened to him in 1940. He couldn't show the manuscript to anyone back then, so he had his sister bury it under a tree."

Mathilde walked for three days and brought back a seashell. It sounded like a fan being opened, a curtain being pulled aside. An action, once decided, simply done.

"Maybe he lied," I said. "About how brave he was."

"I don't think so."

We built the time machine out of twisted bicycle parts and coat hangers and a microwave, and when they took us in, into different interrogation rooms, trying to figure out how, they asked me why. I tried to explain about the radiation scarring and the drowned, but they didn't get it. That's why not everyone can build a time machine. When they left me alone, I leaned my head against the bars and thought of all those times Mathilde and I used to go walking. We lived in a town with no name. We walked across the roofs because there was nothing else left. Only pelicans and frozen waves. She'd ask so many questions.

"What do you do when you survive the last day of your life?"

"How do you go on doing your job after that?"

"How do you decide to keep fighting? Knowing, from personal experience, what comes at the end of the line. How do you risk that, knowing, without going insane?"

"And how do you hold it together when the Gestapo actually gets you a second time?"

"I wonder. Did he believe in God?"

"Was he more or less afraid than the first time?"

"What was he afraid of?"

"Was he more or less brave?"

When Jean Moulin couldn't speak anymore, his torturer gave him a pencil and a piece of paper. Five minutes to write down some names. That guy must've felt triumphant when his prisoner began scribbling furiously. Then it started taking too long. He wasn't scribbling. He was *drawing*.

The torturer tore the paper out of Jean Moulin's hands, only to find a caricature of himself.

"Do you think that really happened?"

"Was it a legend?"

"Was it all made up or partially?"

The time machine brought back: a text message, a handful of dried limes, a clothing line. When Mathilde died—they wouldn't tell me how she did—the time machine stopped working. When they put me in, it wouldn't turn on anymore. So why are you even here, they said.

"What do you think it looked like?" Mathilde asked. "The caricature."

"Probably not too good," I said. "If he'd been tortured to the point where he couldn't speak, he probably couldn't draw too good. It could've been a stick figure with eyes."

But the more she spoke about it, the more I wanted to see it, too. The gloomy climes of 1940s France. It was a miracle anyone lived back then. That anybody could've gone about their days behind rain-washed walls still standing hundreds of years later.

"It's a miracle that Jean Moulin's writing exists," Mathilde used to say, "or we'd have to travel back to get it too. No one would've known about the world he saw. Why did he write? Why did his sister dig it up after the war? Did he write it for her? Did he write it for you and me?"

"Maybe he just wanted to get it off his chest."

Mathilde frowned. She must've been thinking—there's no way someone writes something unless they want someone to read it. Even a bit of graffiti on a Gestapo cell wall. Even if they only see it after you're gone. Even if it's the only thing you've got to look at while you're waiting for the sun to rise, for the pain and silence to start again.

"Was he constantly thinking of ways to die?"

"Did he try to kill himself by banging his head against the walls?"

"What do you think both of them thought when they saw each other?"

"The Gestapo chief and the resistant."

"The torturer and the artist."

"The murderer—"

We can't possibly know what someone thinks when they build a time machine. But I do because I already went through it once before.

"Do you think he was insane?"

"Do you think he was a coward?"

"Do you think he was a martyr?"

When I rebuilt the time machine, I thought about Jean Moulin. Only the idea of him. I drew a finger across my neck. I thought of a scar. The weight of a scarf to hide it all the time. I rebuilt the time machine out of suitcases, syringes, and scrapped airplane parts. I built it out of scraps of paper, scraps of burned paper and stubbed pencils shoved into the hands of people who couldn't speak anymore. I built it out of (love). Then, they couldn't hold me in a cell anymore. I flew across primordial oceans. I perched on a whale skeleton, risen out of frozen waves. I traveled to the Panthéon and laid white roses on the cenotaph of Jean Moulin.

"We can't travel back for art we're not even sure exists," I told Mathilde back then. I regret it now. But that was before I knew how to build a time machine.

Now I can rewrite the conversation:

"Look," I tell Mathilde. And I walk through fields of sunflowers. I walk through an overgrown hillside to a house someone bought before the war because *when the war's over, I don't know what I'll do*; because *I want to turn it into an artist's workshop*; because *when the war's over, I'll just go there and relax.* "Some art exists because it only exists for a moment and only exists for one or two people's eyes. Some art exists because it never existed at all. Just the possibility. They're afraid of us, people like us, the kind of people who can build time machines because we can erase them. They can erase the past, but only we can erase the future. Because they're going to die. Because they don't understand what time is. That's what time is. The possibility—that something exists like the last caricature of Jean Moulin."

THE LEVIATHAN AND THE FURY

It's been over two hundred years since I've spoken to Georges Bidault. But in this timeline, only fourteen. Yet the moment I step into the café, memories sweep over me. I remind myself that he does not invite me to the place where we met after those fateful arrests in 1943 on purpose. He hardly remembers those long meetings over dinner during the war. Discussions about the various resistance movements, their maneuvers and their power struggles, that I only fully understood after reliving them dozens of times. I'm no longer the naïve Free French soldier I was back then. In this timeline, like so many others, I live in Manhattan, where I've become an art dealer. But I know Bidault—prime minister of France, once again—did not invite me to dinner upon my arrival in Paris to discuss that.

"What do you think of de Gaulle's return to power?" he asks me over dessert.

"Absolutely criminal. He should be arrested."

"However, Daniel," Bidault sighs, "this is a crisis. Unchecked, it will be a civil war."

There is always an Algerian Crisis. A metastasis of the Occupation and all the tricks Frenchmen learned from the Nazis, creeping slowly back into the heart of our country again. Bidault chooses to support de Gaulle's presidency, his remolding of the Republic, and it always baffles me. After everything we fought in the war, France doesn't need a dictator. Not even a one-in-a-hundred timeline chance of one. Why does he refuse to see that?

"Of course," Bidault continues, "I would prefer to back someone not quite so . . . that is, someone who could rally the country around himself as well as or even better than de Gaulle. A resistance leader who worked on the ground, tirelessly, to bring all the movements together."

"Frenay, then. Or Brossolette."

"Don't be difficult, Daniel," Bidault says reproachfully. "You know the public adores him, even more so after all his time out of the spotlight. De Gaulle himself agrees with me. But *he* insists the only position he'd be interested in is Minister of Arts and Letters. It won't be like it was in '43. Frenay, Brossolette, all the rest wouldn't dare stand against him. He's more than proven he isn't power hungry . . ."

I stare at a corner of the tablecloth, refusing to take the bait. How could I not have seen this coming? The leviathan lurking in the monstrous depths of my soul has led me into yet another trap. The fury—this desire to leave no branch of any timeline unexplored. Indeed, how can I call it a trap when this conversation is leading to a divergence, a new possibility? My mind drifts to that dinner Bidault and I had together in 1943. After the arrests at Caluire. I'd almost been in tears, since meeting him alone confirmed, irreversibly, our loss. Bidault tried to comfort me in his own way: *Your boss was arrested before. He knows torture. He will do anything to protect us.*

Now, instead, Bidault drones on and on. Until, clearing his throat, he finally caves in:

"You're planning to visit Jean, aren't you?"

"Of course," I answer coldly. "He isn't able to travel as he'd like, as you know, on account of his health. He trusts me to purchase paintings for his gallery. It just so happens that I'm driving out to deliver him one in a few days."

Despite my hints, Bidault's face lights up.

"Then you must ask him. At least convince him to talk to de Gaulle."

"How can I possibly do that?"

"He has a soft spot for you, Daniel," Bidault says, misinterpreting my question. "You were so loyal to him. And then, of course, the Klaus Barbie assassination . . ."

The words nauseate me. It seems so improper to talk of things like Gestapo chiefs and assassinations now that I've lived centuries after the fact. I never wanted to be like the fathers of my generation. Yet I could not have become more like them, wallowing in the miseries of my own Great War. My own trenches. My own shrapnel wounds.

In the Met, there's a painting by Turner that I've probably contemplated more than a hundred thousand times. In the center of the canvas: a whaleboat, a bloody harpoon, flurries of colors only suggesting a monstrous shape. In that painting, I glimpsed my soul. Those I meet over and over again only see the ocean surface of me. Even I've only begun to grasp the leviathan that thrashes beneath—the accumulated fury of thousands of aborted, relived, redone, reconstructed timelines. I can no longer remember the exact number, no longer be disturbed by that fact.

"It's you he owes his life to," Bidault says, smiling. And for a moment, I see the man who was so kind to me at my lowest point in the Resistance, the only one who could share the depths of my grief. "You're going to see him anyway. Please. Just talk to him."

The house in St. Andiol never changes—this red-tiled mas, set against the late afternoon sun. I step out of my rental car, breathing in the scent of lavender. When did I last see it in this timeline? The Moulin family has invited me here often over the years. I never feel comfortable accepting. Just as with all the invitations for Resistance commemorations, ceremonies, and reunions I've left unanswered. I don't want to talk about the past, even with my closest friends. Reliving it is hell enough. But what else can I talk about with my former boss? Every timeline makes him a hero, practically the symbol of the Resistance itself—Jean Moulin.

There is art, I remind myself, glancing at the carefully wrapped painting in the passenger seat. There is always art.

"Dany! I thought that was you. It's been so long!"

Laure Moulin comes around from the back of the house. We exchange greetings, embracing. She's been working in the garden, I see from her clothes.

"Jean's at the studio," she adds. "You'll stay for dinner, won't you?"

I nod, tongue-tied as usual. Laure is a different person from the first timeline I knew her, without her grief. She does not have to say of her brother anymore: *Mocked, beaten, head bleeding, his internal organs ruptured, he attained the limits of human suffering without betraying a single secret, he who knew everything . . .* They don't have to treat me so warmly. They don't owe me anything. Not him, not his sister, not their old mother who thanks me, always, with tears in her eyes. It doesn't escape my notice that neither Laure nor my former boss have children. But if they had, they might've been around my age.

Finally, unable to bear it, unable to put it off any longer, I take my leave of her. It's only a short drive to the bergerie that my former boss converted into a painter's studio after the war. Laure told me that he would often bicycle between it and the house often back in his Resistance days. I can't help but smile, imagining the sight.

The former sheepfold sits on a hillside in the shadow of the Alpilles. The mountains and the long, waving grass look the same as the first time-line I saw them. The Provencal countryside is immutable, it seems. I'm out of breath by the time I make it to the door, the painting under my arm. How does he make it up here every morning? I wonder. I knock three times.

"Come in!"

He sits at a canvas, facing the opposite window. A landscape, but he's not seriously painting—otherwise, he would be outside.

"Three times, Dany? You don't need to knock in code anymore, you know."

"It's a habit," I say. "With you."

"Sit down." He gestures. "I'll be done in a minute. Who knows what I think I'm doing with this painting anyway . . ."

I settle into the indicated armchair, looking around the studio. I helped him fix it up in this timeline. But if I don't, someone else does—he always has plenty of friends. We put in the floor and filled in the cracks in the three walls. The stone of the hill itself forms the fourth, and so the earth, the scent of cypresses and pines, permeates the entire room. Canvases lean everywhere. Landscapes, mostly. A far cry from the contemporary art that's my specialty. Yet I can't help but like them, as I instinctively like all my former boss's work.

"It's terrible, this one," he says offhandedly, dabbing a last spot of color on the canvas. Then he turns around in his chair. "Now. Let's see this painting you've bought me."

Here he is, then. Smiling at me. The man who has haunted my countless lives—Jean Moulin. In another timeline, the original, I became a historian, I wrote ten thousand pages, I did everything in my power to make sure no one would ever forget this man. Is that how I gained this ability? On my deathbed, I drifted off, allowing myself to feel the fury of one who chronicles, helpless to change anything, and the leviathan reared its head . .
.

We talk of the exhibitions I've seen, seen so many times that revisiting them in each timeline is mere formality. I painstakingly unwrap the painting and set it on an easel. He leans forward to examine it. I already suspect what he will say. He, too, is different from the timeline I first knew him in during the war. No trace of the exhaustion that dogged him then remains in his lively, dark eyes. Yet his time with the Gestapo has left its mark. His hair is already beginning to turn white. He is still much thinner than he should be. Even so, he's free from the worry of radio signals from London that I used to code and decode for him, the resistance movement's squabbles, letterbox messages, litanies of meeting requests that I used to bring to him . . .

He speaks of brushstrokes now. Of foam on impressionistic waves.

What right do I have to come here, to disrupt his newfound peace? Yet the leviathan stirs within me. The new path. The new possibility.

"Have you been following the crisis in Algeria?" I venture when our conversation lulls.

Moulin's smile vanishes immediately. But the mischievous gleam in his eyes becomes brighter if anything.

"Did Georges put you up to this?"

I can't hide anything from him. I must say something, make it clear that I haven't come to visit him for just this purpose. But as usual, in moments like these, the words desert me. How is it, even after lifetimes of friendship, that I am still unable to speak my mind?

"Georges has come here many times over the years, trying to convince me to return to politics," Moulin muses. "I suppose he decided to switch tactics."

"He says you won't even meet with the General anymore."

"Let's go for a walk. The sun is going to set soon."

He's turned his head to look out the window again, so I can see the marks running across his neck—faint but still visible. I learned of this scar in another timeline, from a journal his sister buried, from pages that still smelled of tree roots and dirt. Not a wound from the Great War, as I originally thought. But a suicide attempt with a piece of glass in 1940 to avoid giving in under torture . . . faded over the years like my childhood, my adolescence, my Maurrassisme, like everything before the timelines, which always start the day I met him, in 1942.

Moulin rises, pulling on a paint-splattered jacket. He looks a bit like Picasso, who I saw in a restaurant once, like this; if I tell him, he'll laugh. He walks with a limp. The same that prevents him in every timeline from walking down the Champs-Élysées during the Liberation beside the victorious General de Gaulle. Bidault takes his place. I follow, as always, behind with growing trepidation as we edge up the hill.

"I'm not an old man," Moulin says, waiting for me to catch up—that twinkle in his eyes. "Up there is the best place to see the sunset. I want to show you."

Perhaps it's those words, which by their very nature push me to think of him as just that, that kindle the fury always smoldering inside of me. The need to prove to the world why I have such undying loyalty to this man. The need for them to see the same thing I saw the first day I met him, when he saw through me, when he chose me as his secretary, the one who would know all his secrets, putting his life in my hands.

"Why don't you take the position in the government you deserve?" I ask, coming up beside him with a few long strides. "I don't understand why you want to hide away here. France needs you."

He looks at me with surprise.

"Dany, I thought you, of all people, would understand."

Then we're back in the war. Lyon, 1942. Looking over the parapets of the Pont de la Guillotière that would later be blown to smithereens by the retreating Germans. Moulin speaking, or rather monologuing, to me of politics, the resistance movements and old parties, of committees and coordination, and me trying to think of something to say, to show he was right to put his trust in me—and only making a fool of myself. Who am I to criticize his retreat into art? When timeline after timeline after timeline, I've done the exact same thing.

In the original timeline, after Moulin's death, I went to visit the Prado in Madrid because of how often he mentioned it. In the metro, trams, and crowded cafés, whenever people could overhear, he taught me about art. It was our cover story. On that spring morning when the museum was almost deserted, I once again glimpsed him through the paintings, heard him speaking to me. Only then did I realize I was still grieving.

"I'm not like you," I plow on. "You could be the President of a new Republic. You could stand up to de Gaulle."

"Do you think I haven't heard that before?" Moulin says. "They all despised me during the war, but now, to fit in with the myth of the Resistance they've concocted, they adore me. The General wants me to be a Gaullist, the resistance movement leaders want me to support them, and even the communists want to know if I'd like to be their figurehead. I'm a Republican. That's all. I fought for the Republic. Now the Republic has returned."

"But de Gaulle—"

"The General is no dictator," Moulin says firmly. "And—I already gave my life for France. Twice." He eases into his familiar smile. "At Avenue Berthelot, you know, between interrogations, I promised myself that if I survived, I'd live for myself. After the war, I promised myself I'd be done sacrificing. That's the only way I held out for as long as I did."

His words shock me into silence. This is the first time he's spoken of his torture to me. Maybe to anyone. I've never asked. Never wanted to know.

I wonder if I even have the strength to follow as he turns, continuing up the path.

There are certain constants throughout the timelines, things I can never change. I cannot stop him, in 1943, from going to the meeting in Caluire. Cannot stop the betrayal, the Gestapo, the arrest. Cannot stop him from being identified as the most important man in the Resistance. But I can, after hundreds of timelines of trial and error, of downed cyanide pills and firing squads, finally save him. Montluc Prison and Avenue Berthelot are unbreachable. There is only a single opportunity. When the head of the Lyon Gestapo, Klaus Barbie, personally drives his most valuable prisoner to Paris. I learn every possible date. Every possible route. Memorize every single deserted bend in the road.

A few of my Free French companions, carefully sought out and saved from their original arrests, are enough. It's not difficult to convince them: What was all our sabotage training in London for, after all? Someone from my secretariat volunteers to drive the truck, and we swerve to block the road. Klaus Barbie himself always jumps out at the sight. It only takes three shots to end him and his henchmen. A single grenade.

I'm never prepared for the husk of a man I drag from their car.

I don't recognize my boss at first. Blood-soaked bandages swath his head.

His eyes alone show life.

Fifteen years have passed since then. I've relived them hundreds of times. Watched him recover from afar, from across the Atlantic, from his side. He doesn't need my interference. He's always surrounded by family and friends. This, then, as far as I can tell, is as perfect as I can make the rest of his life. What is the sense of repeating it, with slight variation? What am I now trying to find?

Moulin shouts up ahead. I'm going to miss the sunset.

I feel the leviathan within me as I trudge forward. There are so many things I want to say to him—but can't. Despite our lifetimes of friendship, an abyss remains between us. How can I tell him? That when he was arrested, it was the worst day of my life. I felt helpless. The Germans were all-powerful. I'd been orphaned. So certain I'd never see him again. Just like that—I'd lost the man who'd given purpose to my life. Is this God's way of punishing me? Timeline after timeline, for daring to change things? By showing me the inevitabilities?

I crest the path, finally, panting. Wondering, again, how my former boss makes it up here with such ease. Moulin stands with his back to me. He steps closer to the edge, shades his eyes—and stumbles. Without thinking, I close the distance between us, catching him by the arm.

"Maybe I am becoming old," he laments.

He grows still beside me. This, perhaps, is the one scene he's contemplated even more times than I have. Stretched out below us: the little studio, the irrigated fields, the vines—and the sun, setting over a horizon of trees, bathing everything in golden light. I recognize the view from his canvases. The landscape, dozens of angles, and times of day. I cannot remember the last time he painted anything else.

"Sometimes I wonder if they wouldn't all prefer me dead," Moulin says, and a hint of the old exhaustion creeps back into his voice. "As a martyr to use as they pleased, that they could mold into all the things I could never be. That would do more good for the world than any of my paintings . . ."

"Don't say that, Jean."

Does he feel it? I wonder at moments like these. My thousands of lives twined around him, the nexus, the collapsing of space-times. The weight of his original end: the Panthéon, an urn of ashes. A terribly moving speech that calls him *the leader of a people of the night,* that calls him *poor tortured king of the shadows* . . .

All the frustration I've held back for centuries finally bubbles over. Those days in the Resistance passed in slow motion. Day after day, I watched him waste away, beset at all sides by London, the resistance movements, the Gestapo. The first last time I saw him, he looked like he hadn't slept for days. I'd tried to tell him, in my clumsy way, that the noose was tightening. *How can I think of that?* He'd snapped at me. *In a week, we could all be arrested.* Everything I wanted to say back then, when I couldn't save him, between the lines of the thousands of pages of history I've written, the leviathan and the fury, comes pouring out:

"Why won't you just believe we care about you? *You.* You don't have to be a martyr. You don't have to die for the Republic. If you want to spend your life painting, we want you here. But you're not happy here, are you?"

Even now, deep down, he's found no peace. Another constant: He always withdraws after the war. Painting, but even the paintings stop after a while. And always, I stand on the sidelines, unable to do anything but provide a few anodyne afternoons of conversation. Always stretching into silence. He can never know what lies beneath the waves. The inevitability.

But I'm standing right here, hands on his shoulders, talking to him right now, aren't I?

"If you want to do more, then why not return to civil service? Why not talk to Bidault? Why not talk to de Gaulle? Why not become President? Why do you always believe the worst will happen? Even if it happens. We'll be here. I'll be here. You know that."

Moulin doesn't respond at first. He's overtaken with a strange emotion. Serious, but warm too, oddly familiar—then I remember. In winter 1942, just like the original timeline, I nearly froze to death after someone had swiped my coat. He came to visit me as I lay in a safe house, feverishly shivering. *Take care of yourself. I need you.* He gave me a small package wrapped in newspaper. His sugar ration. He had the same expression. Does he remember?

"Then I'll do it," Moulin says, looking up at me. "If you'll be my secretary again."

Is he joking? At times like this, I can never tell.

"We can discuss it over dinner." He's smiling again. "I'm sure Laure will be delighted. Let's hurry back now. Or someone might steal your bicycle."

I redden. The bicycle I'd hit upon the brilliant idea of buying with London's money because it'd speed up my resistance work—stolen within days. Then, the second one, weeks later, along with the coat. He never really forgets anything, does he?

"I have a car now. Well. I rented one."

"Is that so?" Moulin laughs. He turns in the semidarkness to start back down the path, rethinks it. He takes my arm for the first—and I know, last first—time. The leviathan is free now, and after this one has run its course, I will no longer have need of creating timelines.

"Come, Dany. Help this old man down the hill . . ."

ACKNOWLEDGMENTS

Learning to Hate Yourself as a Self-Defense Mechanism (2400 words) – *Clarkesworld* (2022)
Communist Computer Rap God (3100 words) – *Clarkesworld* (April 2021)
There Are No Hot Topics on Whukai (5500 words) – *Lightspeed* (July 2021)
Miss DELETE Myself (5000 words) – *Fusion Fragment* (September 2021)
AIs Who Make AIs Make the Best AIs! (1500 words) – *Fireside* (April 2022)
The Ones Who Got Away From Time and Loss (950 words) – *Nature* (February 2020)
Rebuttal to Reviewers' comments on edits for "Demonstration of a novel Draconification protocol in a human subject" (1400 words) – *Diabolical Plots* (September 2021)
I Want to Dream of a Brief Future (3300 words) – *Aurelia Leo* (May 2020)
And That's Why I Gave up on Magic (1900 words) – unpublished
Resistance in a Drop of DNA (1800 words) – *Clarkesworld* (August 2021)
The Last Caricature of Jean Moulin (1400 words) – *Daily Science Fiction* (2022)
The Leviathan and the Fury (3700 words) – *Asimov's Science Fiction* (2022)

Acknowledgements: Thank you to everyone who has supported my writing over the years. First thank you to my writing professor at MIT, Shariann Lewitt, for introducing me to the world of speculative short fiction and supporting me in all the years since then. Thank you to my writers' groups, who helped make these stories the best they can be: Writer's Block, especially Anna Waldman-Brown, and Codex. Thank you to all the editors and publishers who believed in these stories. A very special thanks to all of my readers, past, present, and future. Last but not least, thank you to guest editor Oghenechovwe Donald Ekpeki, editor Holly Lyn Walrath, and the entire team at Interstellar Flight Press for believing in and publishing this collection. None of this would have been possible without you.

ABOUT THE AUTHOR

Andrea Kriz writes from Massachusetts, where she does research as a molecular biologist. In addition to the stories in this collection, her short fiction has appeared in *Clarkesworld* and *Lightspeed Magazine,* among others, and been translated into French in *Galaxies SF.* She is also part of the Dartmouth Speculative Fiction Project, a collaboration between authors and Dartmouth faculty to create short stories exploring the future of humanity. You can find her online at https://andreakriz. wordpress.com/ or on Twitter @theworldshesaw.

ABOUT THE COVER ARTIST

Dante Luiz is an illustrator and occasional writer from an island in southern Brazil. He's the interior artist for *Crema (comiXology/Dark Horse)*, and his work with comics has also appeared in anthologies, like *Wayward Kindred (TO Comix Press)*, *Mañana: Latinx Comics From the 25th Century (Power & Magic Press)*, and *Shout Out (TO Comix Press)*, among others. Find him online at danteluiz.com

 twitter.com/dntlz

 instagram.com/dntlz

INTERSTELLAR FLIGHT PRESS

Interstellar Flight Press is an indie speculative publishing house. We feature innovative works from the best new writers in science fiction and fantasy. In the words of Ursula K. Le Guin, we need "writers who can see alternatives to how we live now, can see through our fear-stricken society and its obsessive technologies to other ways of being, and even imagine real grounds for hope."

Find us online at www.interstellarflightpress.com.

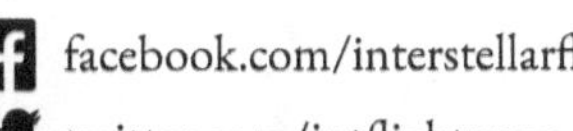

facebook.com/interstellarflightpress

twitter.com/intflightpress

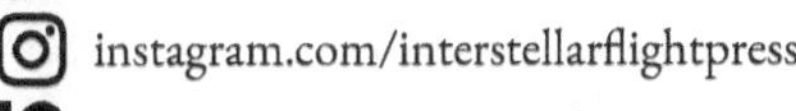

instagram.com/interstellarflightpress

patreon.com/interstellarflightpress